The Grave Listeners

william frank

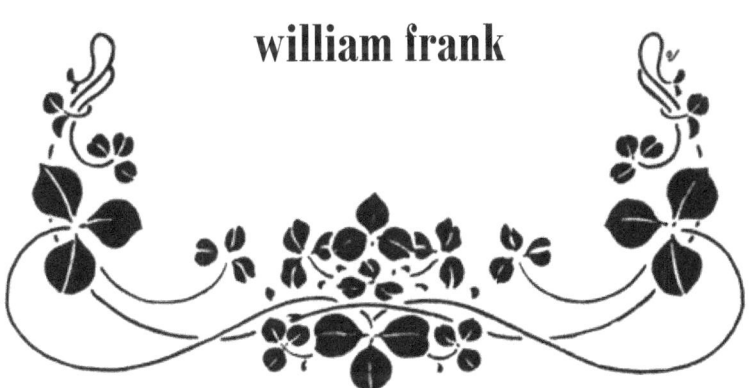

TUCKFORD BUNNY PRESS

ISBN-13: 979-8-9877824-0-8
First Printing: February 12, 2023
Second Printing: November 7, 2023
Third Printing: October 13, 2024
Printed in the United States of America.

Other books by William Frank:

Poetry:
The Shithouse Trouble of Irv Fugman, Deceased (2022)
The Fulgent Requiem (2021)
Slumgullion (2019)
The Purgatory Elm (2018)
Yuneko (2015)
Fiasco Galante (2014)
The Encolpia (2011)
The Morphine Fawn (2009)

All Tuckford Bunny books are available at Amazon.com and other retailers.

About Tuckford Bunny Press
Tuckford Bunny Press is a private, make-believe company that publishes the literary works of William Frank. It is the only imaginary Press that will publish such funny-headed little books.

ACKNOWLEDGMENTS

Floral designs on the Book's Title page, front matter and back cover used from the Permission-Free Designs in the book <u>Art Nouveau Motifs</u>, Dover Publications, Inc., Mineola, NY, 2002.

The Witch's mask in Chapter Six used from the Permission-Free Designs in the book <u>Mythological & Fantastic Creatures</u>, Dover Publications, Inc., Mineola, NY, 2002. The Author modified the facial features in editing software to suit his own idiotic and fantastical purposes.

Grave photos on the Cover and in the front matter created by the author with the gracious help of Marylou Canevari in the midst of a polar vortex at Commack Cemetery in Suffolk County, New York. With sincere love and thanks for the location scouting, set up help and use of your camera and, in the end, for brushing all the leaves and dirt off of me.

The dates on the gravestone were edited by the author to suit the story in an old, atmospheric but non-specific way.

A NOTE FROM TUCKFORD BUNNY PRESS

CONTENTS

❧❧❧❧❧❧❧❧❧❧❧❧❧

You and I must one day die
Shut in a box of pine,
Grant us Mercy we're not sent
Down before our time

Into a dark where eaters creep,
Where none can hear us wail,
Where human nature laughs and weeps
Beyond our fairytales.

The Grave Listeners

1 VOLUSHKA

In an old, poor village, surrounded by a Witching forest, was a cemetery on a hill.

It was early Autumn and at the opposite end of the village, almost all the villagers were hard at work clearing a gap in the trees, collecting the black wood for their winter hearths, for repairing roofs, making Judas Cradles and building new Gallows. By clearing a gap, they could also expand their planting fields for the next season into the meadow beyond, giving room to sow in the Spring the giant *Uphegia* plants that were so important to their survival. The plants grew quickly to heights of 15-20 feet, and the bread-like fruit that hung in clusters from top to bottom provided a starchy, nutritious meal that kept hardy for months, in both hot and cold seasons. The little white blossoms that ran up and down the stalk would be ground into medicines that assuaged headaches, cured hysteria, kept the maggots from a wound; the flowers also made a parfum that blessed a marriage, protected the dead and warded off Witches. Crowning the top of each plant was an enormous cream-colored bell blossom that weighed as much as two pecks of flour and floated in its flocculence on the thick but yielding stalks. The men and the older boys worked away in the wood while the women collected the first fruits and the open white blossoms from last Spring's seeding. The older girls watched over the young children playing in the maze of the *Uphegia*, in the shadows of its broad, black leaves. After lunch, the men would climb to the top of the stalks and tap at the cream-colored crowns to knock them to the ground so that the children could play underneath them, pretending they were houses in their own little bell blossom village.

Not working in the forest and the fields was Volushka, the Grave Listener.

He dozed in his stupefying drunkenness against a headstone, in the cool sunlight in the cemetery on the hill.

Cake crumbs and blossom wine dozed with him on his enormous belly.

On his head was a listening horn that he pulled down over his eyes to shield them from the sunlight (a horn that would in later centuries be used as the horn on Victrola phonographs). Arranged in patchwork all over his body and on his belt were the tools of his trade: a mallet, a flask of alcohol, a spade, candles, a ring of garlic, horseshoe, jack-club, hammer, knife, crucifix, *Uphegia* garland, extra flask of alcohol, a half-eaten, blood-soaked cloth, silver keys and three silver bells. Beside him was a quiver which held long sections of thin metal tubing as well as the stop plate that would be fixed to the lid of the coffin into which the tubes, when assembled, would be inserted. The tubes would stick out of the ground and the horn, when not a hat, would attach to the top so that Volushka could listen for the sound of the poor soul who may have been buried alive.

He just finished listening for five days for the corpse of Father Josep who had a mysterious seizure and danced in delirious convulsions into a bog where he drowned.

Without a village priest nagging at him to respect the dead or sermonizing about turpitude, life in the cemetery was a beautiful, never-ending bounty of peace. Volushka snored in the lazy graveyard under the croaking call of the crows.

Benzi ran up the hill to meet him. He was a little five-year-old boy with impossibly black hair and especially black eyes. He wore the hand-me-down black coat, bowtie and short pants that seven generations of his family's boys wore, and he waved a small butterfly net as he ran around the graves.

When he came upon Volushka, he tickled him with his net. When he got no response, he kicked him in his side.

"What the — Ow! What the Hell is wrong with you?"

"I thought you were dead."

"You don't go around kicking the dead! That's the fastest way to get eaten! I don't have time for you today, what the Hell do you want?"

"Doctor Klaschke needs you."

"So, you came to catch me?"

Benzi waved his butterfly net. "It's for butterflies. And ghosts. It wouldn't be good for you."

"Have you ever seen a ghost?"

"No, but I've seen a giant slob."

"You're about to see a punch in the face!"

"Well, it's a butterfly net, it's not for slobs with a drinking problem!"

Volushka put out his hands as if to strangle him and then instead said quietly, "If you catch a butterfly, it loses all its color. That's how you make ghosts. And to get their color back, they feed on rotten little boys."

"You're also lazy."

"You pain in the ass, you're lazy, and a slob, and just as stupid as those imbeciles down there! What the Hell do you or anybody else know about it? I'm everybody's good-for-nothing until one of their precious loved ones dies, then it's all, 'Volushka, please help us' and 'Volushka, can you please save her?' But they're not precious enough for these people to come up here in the dead of night, in the rain and snow, beset on all sides by ghosts and werewolves, Witches and vampires! How many times have I been attacked by some crazed soul crawling out of the ground who thinks I'm a devil or a meal or otherwise tries to drag me for companionship into the grave? You think anyone can do it? Would you know what to do if you were to meet a Vrykolakas? And what would you idiots know about lazy? I work days *and* nights! I can't afford to go to sleep and miss the sound of someone stirring in the grave! I don't have their luxuries of being cowardly and stupid! They know what it takes? I'm up here preparing, gathering my strength!"

"You looked like you were gathering your fat."

"I have half a mind to slap you in the head!"

"And I have a full mind to punch you in the nose!"

"If you were my kid, I'd raise you right and drown you in a well."

"I'd drown myself. And you smell like shit."

"You rotten — get out of here and don't come back!"

"Ok, but Doctor Klaschke wants you."

"Why?"

"My mother's on his table."

Volushka and Benzi walked side by side out of the cemetery and down the street. As they walked, Volushka kept doing an equipment check, patting himself down, while settling the listening horn on his head. Benzi mimicked him by adjusting his little black bowtie and smoothing his hair. As they approached the Undertaker's,

Benzi ran on ahead, waving his net. The Undertaker emerged in the doorway and snapped his fingers at Benzi in a command to come to him, but Benzi just stopped and stared at him, waiting for Volushka to catch up. The Undertaker sneered at Volushka.

"Always trying to hang on to a last hope. And God damned it, you're it. It sickens me to think these poor people are paying for nothing but a damned excuse for you to drink up there."

"A family has a right to be sure."

"If they left it to me, they'd be perfectly sure. I don't much appreciate having to dig it up after a week to show the incredulous family a face-folded corpse with all the bugs crawling out of its nose nor do I enjoy arguing about refunds in the admittedly rare instance you're sober enough to do your job and pull some scrambled lunatic out of the ground. Be a sensible idiot and call this one right."

"When I was in Klovokstrad, the town warder asked me to listen for a woman who, we later saw, swallowed the keys to the grain reserve just for spite so that it spoiled her belly and she died. Or *seeming* died, for when I heard her screaming and they dug her out, she stood straight up, ran over to the granary and unlocked the door. There were claw marks all over the inside of the coffin and clumps of hair everywhere; there was blood all over her face and her graveclothes from disgorging the key. And when they beat her up, they noticed that half her fingers had been eaten off. But if that had been someone you'd loved, you'd have wished for a surety. They wanted me to be their permanent Grave Listener but they had a famine, so I left."

"I wish we had a famine."

"You need a good Grave Listener. A town quickly gets out of balance without one and then there's corruption in all places."

"If you don't dig them up, they die or they're dead, all the same. Tell them at Klaschke's: they have to pay me first despite whatever nonsense you're going to do up there."

Volushka and Benzi continued to the Doctor's home. When they arrived, they stood at the door. Benzi waited with him while Volushka prinked with a regal air.

"When you die, who's going to listen for you?"

"I don't know. Like I said, it's not something anyone can do. You have to be able to discern, scientifically, between the natural, the supernatural and the subtleties of the imagination. You have to have a fine ear. You can't just walk into a town and say, 'I'm a Grave Listener, who's dead, I'll have a listen.' You have to be haunted. I've known men who have done just that and made a mess of it. You know what the punishment is for fraudulent listening? Having hot bars driven into your ears. Try combing your hair after that. No, it takes a professional, connected soul and a keen sensitivity."

The Nurse glowered at the window. "Are you two just going to stand out here?!"

"What?"

"Don't make me shout again, there's grieving inside. The Doctor's waiting for you." She slammed the window closed.

Volushka huffed. "When I die, make sure you burn my head down to the ashes."

"I'm not allowed to get dirty."

They entered and Volushka removed his Victrola hat, respectfully, as Benzi's grieving family eyed him cautiously. Seated around the parlor were Benzi's Aunt and Uncle, his two older sisters and his Grandmother. Benzi ran to his Aunt and caught her hands in his butterfly net and then his eldest sister gathered him into her lap. Volushka removed a white blossom from his *Uphegia* garland and approached Benzi's Aunt with a solemn, aristocratic air. Benzi's Uncle sneered.

"I am sincerely sorry for your predicament."

"We just want an honest assurance," his Aunt replied.

"I'm sure you do. Is that because you've poisoned her?"

"Certainly not!"

"What the Hell is wrong with you?" shouted the Nurse.

The Uncle leapt from his seat. "Get the Hell out of here! We don't need you!"

"I'm sorry, I'd love to be delicate and mince all around the room but in my business, I don't have the time or the luxury to indulge your cosmopolitan niceties! If you botched it, there's a very good chance she'll wake, I need to know the facts right up front, for my own protection! I will be the first person the monster sees and I have to know if it's going to be sad, insane and murderously angry. Now, was she prone to lunatic, farting rampages?"

The Uncle grabbed him by his throat. "I'll kill you, you stupid ass!" They wrestled and tumbled into a table, knocking a bowl of flowers to the floor, shattering it. They then crashed all around the room to the screaming of the Aunt, the sisters and the Nurse as they all dodged the brawl. Benzi's Grandmother simply folded her hands. The Doctor came in and kicked both men to separate them.

"That's enough! That's it! Enough! You, come inside!"

The men were parted and Volushka, who seemed to get the worst of it, looked confused and unsteady, his pants right around his knees. He pulled one side of his pants up, collected his Victrola hat from the floor and staggered into the examination room. The Nurse and Doctor followed. Benzi broke away from his sister, picked up a flower from the broken bowl and ran to the examination room door as it closed on him.

The Nurse began washing the body again as Volushka pulled himself together. The Doctor sat on a stool watching him with tired disgust. When Volushka cleared his head and readjusted all his kit, he approached the body.

"Any livor mortis?"

"She's dead. Let's not have a whole affair. Just sit here for a little while, have a drink and then go out there and pronounce it."

"I'm also hungry."

"This isn't a tavern. Don't prolong the suffering, we don't need it. One procession up the hill, and just leave it where it is."

"It's important to know."

"I already know. I'm a doctor."

"So, why don't *you* tell them? What did you call me for if you're such a damned authority?"

"I did tell them. It's the Grandmother."

"Well, then I'll work."

Volushka re-entered the parlor and Doctor Klaschke followed peevishly and stood in the door. Volushka approached Benzi's Aunt and took her hand. She recoiled for a moment but then allowed him to hold it. He looked at the Grandmother and then back to the Aunt.

"I reviewed the figment, and it looks to me like it could go either way. From the coloration and the girth, it seems she could be retaining a little life, what we call Supraliminal Living, undetectable by most authorities. Of course, unless you're Death, no one in the whole world can say for sure and it may be better to accept that she's dead. But I saw a reunion once in Poldostoka that makes me believe you should consider the chance. I know choosing can be hard, and all the worry, and I know she's worried about you. For a little less, I can crush her skull…"

Benzi's Aunt gasped and removed her hand from his.

"…She won't remember it. It should only take one or two really big swings. I know it's not about the money, but I can provide a kind of peace. I'll let you think about it."

Benzi's Grandmother said calmly, "We'll take your service. I don't want her to pass away shut in a pit."

"Yes, it's a dark, suffocating pit. I can listen for three nights, for five nights or for ten, including Sabbaths. I get three meals and three bottles of liquor per day…"

"One bottle!" the Uncle snapped.

"I take three bottles, it gets cold at night! And I want meat or fish and some kind of pie not just gruel or millet, I'll just come back otherwise. I want a new shawl and a good ration of tobacco for me and for her."

The Uncle rose out of his seat ready to swing. "Why does she need tobacco?!"

"You're getting a man of experience for a very delicate responsibility! It's not just daydreaming! For one, I blow the smoke down the tube and I try to make her cough. I have a whole congregation of methods. Ten dolmarks a day for three days, eight a day for five days and six for ten, half up front for three and five days, half up front for ten with half of the remaining brought on the fifth day. I work alone and don't want anybody watching me or visiting or otherwise distracting me, except for the ones who bring me food and I won't otherwise answer any questions or give any notes until I am done. You'll have to petition the town to be quiet, that no work or loud divertissements be performed, and you'll have to pay the expenses thereof, if any, or else I provide no guarantees. I also charge for a bath and a woman when I return so as to shake off the business of Death and I don't negotiate that."

"Doctor Klaschke, is there any chance?" the Aunt implored.

"No."

"Then at least bury her with some bread and a mirror so she won't be lonely. Good afternoon, and I'll be sorry for your nightmares." Volushka bowed, doffed his Victrola hat and made a wide path around the Uncle to leave.

"We'll take the service at three days," Benzi's Grandmother said.

"That should be enough, I guess."

She paid him. The Uncle then gestured to his wife to follow and brusquely exited. The Aunt tried to bring Benzi with her, but he resisted and cuddled to his sister. The Aunt then followed after her husband, somewhat embarrassed. Volushka then addressed the Grandmother.

"Bring all of these to the Undertaker and he'll bore a hole in the coffin lid and nail this stop plate to it with the neck facing up. He'll screw these tubes together and then attach them to this part here. Tell him I said that, when he buries around the tube, make sure that this time it's sticking out at least twenty inches above the ground and fetch me when she's covered. I'll be at the brothel."

2 THE LAZY REQUIESCAT OF AFTERLIFE DAYS

The Funeral procession worked its way slowly down the hill to return to their hard village life, first in order and then breaking up in all directions, the old, discarded sexton tolling the Church bell the whole afternoon until the villagers absolutely had enough and forced him to stop.

When the burial was finished, Benzi disappeared into the brothel and then emerged with Volushka to see him off to his mission on the hill. Pinned onto Benzi's lapel was a white butterfly. Pinned onto Volushka's lapel was a new blossom wine stain. He patted Benzi on the head who then punched him in his knee. Benzi ran off down the street waving his butterfly net.

At the new grave, the tube was sticking out of the ground like a blown away dandelion. Next to the tube was a small pinwheel whose little bells tingled in the wind. It was sunny on the hill but felt a little cold, so Volushka was glad to see the three big jugs of blossom wine leaning against the small, temporary wood marker. He stretched himself up and scratched himself before wrapping his new shawl around him tight. He swept the sand around with his feet to make a flat, comfortable spot to lay down and then took a gentle swig off the blossom wine. He took a big, satisfying breath of the cool, autumn air and luxuriated in the sunlight on his face. He then struck the tube with his mallet once to be sure it was in place and attached the Victrola horn to it. He listened at it for a minute and then settled down to take a nap.

He woke after a couple of hours with the clouds drifting as lazily by. He rolled up some tobacco and settled into a nice smoke, humming a half-formed tune in his head as the smoke curled listlessly around him. Leaves jumped up in the little bursts of wind that were the wakes of dancing ghosts. He daydreamed about the bath at the end of his service and the fine old time he would have back at Petchka's brothel, the soft downy beds on the second floor and the equally fluffy body of Magaden who, like everyone else, hated his guts. Thinking that there was no sense getting himself all worked up now, with three days left, he drifted into a little fish pie, a new smoke and a revery of peace.

The cemetery wrinkled with the perfume of the grass, the flutter of butterflies, the caw of the crows. Flowers left at the different graves dotted the hill with bright announcements of color. Here and there, a chipmunk darted around the graves. Volushka filled the air with various shapes of tobacco smoke, pleased with his ingenuity in his beautiful rivalry with the clouds. His relaxed, sleepy eyes shuffled through the shifting images of a turtle, a manticore, a ruff, a lady bending over. As the smoke thinned and vanished, as if by rite, the clouds conjured there a man standing directly over him with a dashing, kindly face. Volushka started and sat up.

"It's like the Hell of the Blessed Pagans up here, isn't it? Nothing to do but be dead or just loll around and smoke. Sorry, I didn't mean to astonish you, I just couldn't help noticing how peaceful it all seems. My name's Marcabrusa, mind if I sit down with you? I've been walking for days. …Everybody's resting, the poor dears. You probably don't get much company like me up here anyway."

"In fact, I do mind. I'm working."

"As what, fertilizer?"

"It's none of your business what I do!" Volushka put his hand on his long knife and stood up.

"A strange business at that; if you can make a living at it, I commend you all the same. What I wouldn't give to be in your profession! I'm an everyday laborer myself, pike driving, blacksmithing, farm work, timbering, whatever I can get. I don't look like much, being so handsome, but I'm strong where it counts. Men should look out for me. And ladies, too. But I'd be very glad to put down in a peaceful situation."

"This is about as peaceful as it can get." Volushka now menaced with both his mallet and the knife.

"Then again, I'm also something of an intellectual, an astute observer of nuance and bristling with a joy for life. It's amazing how all of this, the big and small, the seen and unseen, the living and the dead, are so interconnected but still so secretly amuck, like a clout on the head. But it seems that's just inviting a comparison, to be avoided, and I'm boring you. Is there any other work around? Or could you recommend a place to eat?"

"The village is at the bottom of the hill. But they're not as friendly to strangers as I am."

"No village is, I expect. But I'm grateful for the warning. Good-bye my friend, I wish you all success in your Paradise of cemeteries, this beacon on a hill."

He watched Marcabrusa disappear beyond the graveyard with his annoyingly joyous spirit.

He sat down at the grave and pulled the pinwheel from

the ground. Interrupted by this smug intruder and still bristling at the fertilizer remark, the cemetery now seemed gloomy. He took another draw on the blossom wine and tried taking a nap but the sting of being discovered as a layabout pricked him into work. He blew some smoke down the horn and listened, but it all seemed like a hollow void. He brought some food up to the horn to entice the corpse with the smell and then realized he was hungry and sat in the dust to eat.

When night fell, the cemetery came alive. The quiet of the village below brought all the noises of the graveyard into focus. Everywhere was the presence of Witches and vampires, and they hovered in the little stand of trees at the back of the hill opposite the graveyard gates. The wolves baying to the waning moon seemed to move closer in the darkness and with a desperate, hungry urgency in their cries. The ground itself seemed to move, beyond the forces of the ululating wind or the crawly, biting bugs, as if something were trying to breach from underneath. He felt an especial cold in his bones, despite how early in autumn, a cold that came with its own voices. Every snapping twig was an imminent attack, faces appeared and disappeared all around him, in the fungus on the tree, or in the shadows on the stones. Devils shook the blossoms on the bushes and the sound of vast cohorts of unfamiliar beasts made their ghastly chorus to the powers of the air.

He thought about how his ancestors died before, mighty and brave Grave Listeners all of them, in their spectacular fight between Good and Evil: his great-great-grandfather, Voluskavuc, at the hands of a prostitute who died underneath him at the brothel who later burst out of her grave with a furious animal strength, despite being nailed to the coffin floor. Voluskavuc's son, who was pulled into the grave of a returning vampire escaping the dawn, was then fed upon throughout the day in the coffin and emerged the next night as the undead. His head was cut off and nailed to the rafter of the brothel where he was captured while feeding on Hilga Kosokoya, the Marsh town girl. His grandfather, Volusjalic (a Grave Listener so feared and respected, he was once called to listen at the tomb of the Lord of the Lurids himself) who was eaten by an empusa that then dragged his hollowed body out from the cemetery and hid it under the porch of the brothel. His father, who never truly recovered from his battle with a family of four who clawed their way out of their graves while he was sleeping, died of drink and syphilis, most likely from the brothel. He thought about hiding in the village for the three days and wondered about who was up at the brothel.

The three days and nights passed like a spinning wheel of fright, boredom, drink, weather, and madness. He lolled about in the fresh sunlight, he felt sorry for himself under the disappearing moon; he wrinkled pleasantly at noon, smoothing his bare feet in the grass, and he pined pitifully in the lashing night rain. He threatened the ghosts in his confident strength in the daytime, he cowered behind a gravestone surrounded by the howling dark. Soft Maidens emerged from his imagination in the air and when they brushed his face, decayed into ghastly, ravenous monsters. A vampire watched him from the trees. He drank himself into stupors and he spent the dawn of the second day looking for his pants among the graves. Time ticked away like a sad little luxury, the only graveyard thing more shiftless than Volushka. The beautiful little cemetery crowded him somberly with all manner of enticements and threats, far above the world in its confusing solitude on the hill.

Life here had its own mysterious gulf where everything

could be accomplished by the spiders and worms and sunshine, the flowers, the clouds and spectres.

In the dawn of the third day, Volushka walked down the hill dirty and tired, yawning and scratching his beard as he approached the Grandmother, the Aunt and Benzi's sisters waiting for him anxiously at the gate. As he caught up even with them, they asked wordlessly through their searching, worried expressions, "Well?" and without stopping he shook his head No.

3 MARCABRUSA

Volushka went to Petchka's and banged at the door. The girls were all only a couple of hours into sleep and the quiet dawn village, peopled only with ghosts and mists and silence, made Volushka feel like the graveyard was following him. The shivers made him bang on the door again with fever and insistence.

Petchka finally roused, opened the door, and punched him in the face.

"Dammit! Every time! Why?!"

"Because you're a filthy idiot! You should be hanged and thrown in the cess pit!"

"I've got money."

"It's dawn, we're closed! Everyone's sleeping, the girls have a right to sleep! Now get out of here before I kick your balls up to your neck! You make me sick."

"And you're so high and regal, with talk like that. I have half a mind to knock you out, since it won't make a difference in your estimation of me."

Petchka punched him in the face again. She then kicked him like she said she would.

"O God! I just... for God's sakes! ...I just came back from Grave Listening! ...ow. I just want a bath and a place to lay down. I have some money. When everybody's up, I want a girl, I won't get out of line and I'll pay you right. It's awful up there in that cemetery."

"Well, I don't want you bringing it in here. It's a disgusting business."

"And prostitution is some noble institution?"

"How dare you! Get out of here!"

"I'm not judging you, I'm here, aren't I? I'm just noting that we all have to make a living as best we can. And I'm just looking to pay for a little kindness. Here's a halfmark for waking you up. I'm sorry. I'll be quiet, I promise."

"There's a tub out back, I'll leave some lavender at the door. You stay out there until we're ready and then, if I can convince anyone to stomach you, and that's going to take some money, I'll send for you."

Petchka slammed the door in his face.

Volushka sat in the cold bath behind the brothel watching the dawn convoke the day. He was alone and miserable. The ghosts were back in the graveyard but the people were in the village. He suffered in his lavender.

After his bath, he sat for hours behind the brothel trying to draw the smoke out of the last leaves of his tobacco, waiting for Petchka. He was impatient but afraid to press, reminded by his testicles of her powerful right leg and her chthonic tempers. He once battled a Blemmyae in Tolvoskya (and in a drunken haze no less) but he knew enough not to tangle with her.

Despairing for a long time about his chances and about to wander away, Rutchka came to the back door and motioned him to come inside. She was a sturdy, jowly girl with a perpetually aggravated expression who wore a pigtail off the side of her head like an angry root. She was the only girl who had the constitution to sleep with him; she was known to sleep with incurables, lunatics, the condemned and werewolves and looked you right in your face as you did it. Volushka hated her guts as much as she hated his. He followed her inside.

After he slogged through an hour with Rutchka, who wouldn't get off him no matter how much he pleaded, he took another bath, ate a small plate of fish stew and staggered out of Petchka's into the street. Benzi was waiting there for him, replacing the butterfly net with his lifelong companion, a ratty, grey stuffed Bunny rabbit with eyes as black as his own and a vacant Bunny rabbit expression. Volushka would often threaten to kick the Bunny rabbit in the face, which made Benzi laugh, and this infuriated Volushka, who couldn't ever seem to upset this infernal, pain-in-the-ass child.

"What are you two doing here?"

"Waiting for you."

"Well, I don't have time to be hanging around with you, I've got a lot to do."

"Getting lumpy isn't a lot to do."

"I'm not doing this with you right now! I spent three days looking after your mother surrounded by Hell figures, I don't have the reserves. Shouldn't you be home mourning?"

"What's that?"

"What do you mean, what's that? Being sad, that's what, haven't you ever been sad?"

"No."

"Are you some sort of goblin child? How is that even possible?"

"Because I don't want to get stupid and gross like you."

"Get over here so I can smash your face!"

"You get over here so I can smash your entire head!"

"I'm going to pick you up and throw you through that brothel window!"

"Jesus couldn't pick you up without destroying his pelvis!!"

"You son of a — you rotten little imp!"

Volushka grabbed Benzi and they started wrestling, lifting Benzi off the ground, and they spun as they rumbled, with the little boy with the black eyes laughing, cuddling his Bunny and eventually biting Volushka as he called Benzi all sorts of curses. The rumbles only came to a stop when confronted by the stern Mrs. Wlawicka.

"You let that boy go, you animal, before I call the men to kick your head down the street! Can't you see that boy is in mourning?"

"This isn't a boy, he's a flagrant ulcer! The only mourning this boy knows about is the one he inflicts!"

"How dare you! He's an angel with feet! You come here, Benzi, and stay away from that awful thing!"

"Yes, Mrs. Wlawicka."

"That's a good boy, he's such a good boy. As for you, why don't you kill yourself!"

"You don't know anything about it so why don't you mind your own business, you harridan! They ought to burn you alive, you old Witch!"

Mrs. Wlawicka picked up a stone and threw it at him.

"Get out of here, you animal! I'm going to call the men!" She led Benzi away, smoothing his hair as the Bunny stared knowingly at Volushka over Benzi's shoulder, his ears flopping as they went.

He decided not to wait around for the men to come and beat him up and wandered down the dusty dirt street until he came to the little pie shop of Mrs. Jarmulka, where a crowd had gathered. Sitting on a barrel was Marcabrusa, holding forth and trying to win over a throng at once captivated by him and suspicious. Volushka stood off to the side, at the beginning of the adjacent alley, in case he had to run from the crowd he himself had lost long ago.

"…Well, of course, that's a few of the more extraordinary places I've seen but I'd love to settle down here. You sure have a nice cemetery. I've been to a lot of villages that didn't and down to the last child they've been a mean-spirited lot."

"Well, don't think we aren't, especially to vagabonds who expect to just drink and lay about and cause mischief around here."

"You wouldn't find that with me, I have all kinds of trades. I was a person that was sought out in my last village whenever the job had to get done, and I was always glad to lend support for a moral cause. And it was a nice place, too. That was a group of people you could admire and love, a rare living, indeed."

"So why didn't you stay?"

"Wanted to very much. Loved a woman there of the best virtue, prettiest thing you've ever seen, unequalled for industry and sweetness, the present ladies excepted, but she passed away and for the grief, I almost quit the village and, alas, the world."

The women looked at each other modestly and sighed for such a notion.

"You cherished her memory too much?"

"I couldn't cherish it enough."

The men, losing their women to this handsome jongleur, were understandably suspicious and most likely murderous.

"You cherished her memory so much, you just got up and left it behind?"

"I would have left it all behind, I was torn in half spiritually. I lost my better part. I think some of the ladies here can understand what I mean when I say spiritually and therefore, for grief of love, I thought about ending my life to join her, so that I may enter our eternal bond together. It is only because she came to me from beyond in a dream to prevent me from committing that terrible sin, an act that would have separated us forever, that I preserved my soul. I dedicated each day in the village to hard work, clean living and quiet devotions so that I could honor her. But then the plague came."

The crowd gasped and a thrill of fear rose up in every person. Frightened glances, the gabble of shock, swells of panic and spells of near fainting gripped the villagers, who searched frantically in their neighbors' faces for any sign of sickness.

"I stayed as long as I could and I helped where I was asked – I guarded shut-up houses, I burned clothes and keepsakes, I buried the dead. In the end, we had been overcome. And I alone escaped to tell thee, alas."

The men took the opportunity to recover their places. "You people better get back, you don't know if he's infected!"

"You don't know anything about this man!"

"You better run him off!"

"I appreciate your concern, believe me…"

"We ought to kill him for the risk of it!"

"Friends, I lived through it and saw its worst, so your suspicion is a completely natural and understandable reaction. I realize now that the men in this village are sensible and sober in their judgment and it's the blessing of every man to live in a village like this one that's guided by moral reason and neighborly concern. I come as a friend, beseeching your Christian charity, but in the end, I'll leave if you want. If you'll simply allow me to say, I absolutely assure you that I am almost supernaturally well. I am young and strong, and if an upright and honest matron would care to inspect me, you'll find no blemish on any part of me. I've simply never felt better."

He leapt off the barrel and pirouetted with a lithe, animal grace, stretching his limber body to its full height, throwing his head back until his bangs settled winkingly over one of his eyes, to the palpitating delight of the upright and the honest.

"A sensible village could certainly be forgiven for driving me out, since I am a stranger, even as our Lord reminds us not to neglect our hospitality to strangers, for in their hospitality some have entertained angels unawares. But, friends, I take to heart the same obligation as a stranger to be an upright and Christian guest. If I thought I was a hazard in any way, especially to the good ladies of this village, who so remind me of my own departed beloved, why, if I thought I could harm them even to the little end of their fingers, it would be such an unbearable violation to me that I would take my own life to save them, even to my eternal separation from my darling Nitchka, for I would no longer deserve her. I would *never* have entered your village if I thought for a moment that I was a danger to you, conscious of my moral duty to your welfare, as I would expect a good Christian people to not willingly or unjustly do any harm to me. My only hope is that you'll give me the chance to show you that I am a man of good conscience. I desire nothing more.

"Now, if I *was* sick, I couldn't hide it and that's the truth, for this plague was very terrible and strange. There were ghastly, swollen buboes that burst and issued a foul, black pus, with a bloody, unrelenting cough that burned through your insides. People tore out their hair, and at their skin, in the torment of its violent ague. If you had it, you often perished fast — a stout man could have breakfast in the morning in the full glow of his strength and by supper be dead, covered in great black boils and scalded with fever.

Whole households would vanish in a moment and street by street the plague would take all of its neighbors. It gave an eeriness to the whole place, people lying all about, some with their eyes open and their tasks half done, their jaws open where, like as not, a mouse ran in. You didn't have much chance once you felt a spell to have gotten very far, even from your house to the church door, let alone to the next village. I promise you I could not be standing here if I had this plague, for I would have been consumed in an instant as if by Hellfire. No one knows the time or the scope of this sickness, nor the judgment of God, but I have seen it and I have survived it, delivered by God's Grace and the goodness of His Mercy."

Many long, uneasy looks and whispers circulated among the fascinated crowd, gangs of frightful spectres threatened to break into conflagratory hysteria. Marcabrusa gave them an easy smile.

"While you consider my fate and all of God's works, if you don't mind, I am going to rest for a while in the tavern and if any of you would like to come and share some food and drink with me, I would be grateful for your company. I can tell you about the village I passed through just before I came here, perhaps you know them, there just beyond those marshes? They were the worst, so unlike you in every conceivable way, it is hard to believe the villages are so near to each other. I am almost ashamed to share any accounts of their strange and depraved customs, the monstrosities of which may owe to the corrupting effects of the marsh gases that shroud them in the dead of night, but I may put aside my restraint and propriety to recount for my dear friends their awful grotesqueries. It's as dreadful as you'd like."

The crowd broke into gales of laughter, exchanging knowing looks while regaling each other with tales of their backward neighbors, aping their animal gait, their horrendous assfaces and flatulent stupidity. The men gabbled their way to the tavern with Marcabrusa, the women cachinnated to Mrs. Gogostoika's

Volushka could see this man was a natural enemy and needed to be dealt with *in extremis*. He was especially worried that Marcabrusa would disclose all he saw when they met in the cemetery and tell them his stupid fertilizer joke. A man who is a sparkling conversationalist and has all his teeth is a pernicious danger to all that meet him.

After the street cleared and Volushka was finally able to muster the courage, he went in to join them so he could monitor what Marcabrusa was saying and counter any aspersions levelled against him. As expected, the convivial room fell silent when he entered and sneers even came from the ceiling. Marcabrusa greeted him fulsomely.

"Well, there's my happy friend! Rested and pert! I was wondering when I'd see you again. I wanted to thank you for recommending this village, you were right about the tavern."

"You know this shithead?" Lusbek, the tavern keeper, asked.

"He introduced me to your cemetery, he was keeping its flowers in bloom."

"Well, he's about to join them," Big Rheinskold said, glaring at Volushka. The animus quickly spread to the other villagers.

"He and his family have been a curse on the place for generations."

"The whole place stinks with them."

"We ought to take him out back!"

"I don't know this stranger," Volushka said as he took a step back to the door. "He came at me in the cemetery and I put him to flight. I thought I ran him out but like a devil he came back. We don't know about this man, what plague is with him, what evil!"

"We know about you, you good for nothing, piece of shit."

"Look at him, it makes me sick!"

"There's always some idiot walking around here in a moron costume."

"Always jangling around!"

"Like a clown!"

"Like a peddle cart!"

"Jangle! I said Jangle, you idiot!"

Volushka desperately tried to hold the crowd as Marcabrusa drank placidly among them. "Listen, he's trouble! The Prince of Lies! You don't know what he's bringing on you! Consider your women!"

"Dance, you piece of shit!"

"Let's hear you jangle!"

They chased Volushka into the street and surrounded him, pushing him around the circle, slapping him in the head and shouting at him to dance. Little children joined the circle to throw rocks at him while the village laughter carried everywhere on the wind. The women stopped their work and came, too, clapping in time to make the music of the dance as Volushka tried to crash through different parts of the circle but was thrown back each time into a heap in the center. The singing and clapping, the cursing, the gibes and the laughter rose until, at its tipping height, the circle closed in and they kicked him and beat him and clubbed him until he was unconscious.

They then tore off all the kit he wore around his body, the mallet, the flask of alcohol, the spade, the candles and garlic, the horseshoe, jack-club, hammer and knife, the crucifix, the *Uphegia* garland, the bells, the tubing and the horn, and they threw them everywhere in the street.

4 A TIME FOR GRAVE LISTENING

At the bottom of a little dip to the left of the *Uphegia* fields was an old, long, gnarled up log on which Volushka would often sit to nurse his wounds, to rant about life and pity himself.

And despite his most earnest wishes to the contrary, Benzi and his Bunny were always beside him on the log to help.

"Your face looks stupid."

"Your face looks stupid! Why don't you go home, I don't have the strength right now!"

"There's nothing to do at home. And your face looks disgusting, like a pie that fell on the floor!"

"Thank you."

"And a horse shit in it."

"Ok, that's it! I've got a headache, can't you go someplace and kill yourself?"

"Yes."

"Well, then why don't you?"

"Because I'm *so bored* and you'll probably do something funny. You know, everyone will probably come back and beat you up."

"Well, let them! I'll kill the lot of them!"

"Why didn't you beat them up before?"

"I could have easily beaten up every one of them! I once beat up ten guys from a regiment in Novokanska who insulted the honor of a Principessa! There must have been about a hundred people back there!"

"And some children."

"I'm not the kind of animal that beats up children!"

"That's because you can't."

"I beat up lots of children!"

"I saw a kid kick you right in your face!"

"Lots of people were kicking me in the face, I had dirt in my eyes, I had already beaten up about fifty people, my fists were getting tired!"

"Your face didn't seem to be getting tired, you just sat there looking blobby and getting kicked in the head!"

"And you think you could have done any better?!"

"I could beat up five hundred people!"

"So, go beat them up! Just leave me alone!"

"Aren't you always alone?"

"No, I've got this little monster who keeps sticking me with his awful knife!"

"Ooo, can I see him?!"

"No, you — it's you, are you being dense on purpose?!"

"No, are you shaped like shit on purpose?"

"Do you want to go toe to toe with me?"

"Do you want to go toe to toe with *me*?"

"You're about to be in a whirlwind of fists!'

"I'm about to be in a whirlwind of fat!"

"I'm going to punch you into kingdom come, you little brat!"

"I'm going to punch you into the sky!"

"Kingdom come is farther than the sky."

"No, it isn't."

"Yes, it is!"

"No, it isn't."

"IT IS SO! How would you know, you little rat?"

"Everybody knows except you!"

"You know what, I'm not arguing with a precocious imbecile! Is everything in this place possessed?"

"Yes."

"You are the most impish thing on earth! Your family must want to disembowel themselves!"

"They love me just like God loves me."

"Then they must want to bash your head in — God hates nasty little boys!"

"Obviously, that's why He loves me."

"God wants to punch you in the face!"

"God punches you in the face all the time!"

"When God looks at your face, He kills a puppy!"

"If anyone looks at your face, they'll throw up and their eyeballs will fall out!"

"You know what, I don't care, I'm not talking to you! …O God, now who is this idiot?"

Climbing down the little slope was the Undertaker.

"I don't know why you're always hanging around with this little boy but you're going to get killed if you corrupt him in any way. How many times do you have to get punched in the face to get any good sense?"

"First of all, this is not a little boy, it's a sixty-five-year-old woman with cramps. Secondly, *he's* always hanging around with *me!* Every time I turn around, he just magically appears out of some Hellmouth!"

"I don't really care what happens to you, to be honest, I'm telling you for the boy's sake. If I have any concerns about your welfare, it's only because I'd miss the entertainment of watching you get the shit kicked out of yourself all the time. That was a wonderful display back there."

"Well, I'm glad to go one-on-one right now, let's see how tough you are without a hundred of your friends with you!"

"Don't try it. You know better."

"I'll try it, wait until the swelling goes down around my eyes and I'll hit you with a couple of quick ones that'll take your head off!"

"I'm over here. Look, I don't want to be around you longer than is necessary, while you were busy being mauled beef, Mrs. Makovöd's daughter died under mysterious circumstances and the villagers have now sent me to fetch you."

"Oh, really, isn't that something? Now, everyone wants my help and none of them have the courage or the decency to come and ask me themselves! The gall, the living gall! I tried to warn them that that stranger was bringing a whole lot of trouble with him but they're all eating and drinking and having a good time together! Well, they can all go to Hell! I'm not doing it!"

"He's under suspicion, too, and the villagers are in a frightened, vengeful mood. You better really think hard about not going up there."

"What do you mean "too," why am I under suspicion?!"

"Because you're an asshole."

"Is that right? Well then, they're not going to want an asshole to help them with their very serious problem, somebody more popular better get in the coffin with her to make sure she doesn't wake up alone down there!"

"You really are stupid, aren't you? I'm glad to tell them you've refused, they're not going to kill you quickly, they're going to beat you, burn you and otherwise torture you to death for their own animal entertainment. You're nothing to these people, you're alive for the one disgusting thing that you do. And Marcabrusa has offered to listen for the girl, to show his earnest concern and to try and stave off their anger; among all his other superior qualities, he obviously has a better sense of self-preservation than you."

"What?? He's not a Grave Listener! He can't do that! He's a fraud, they need to arrest him and maim him! It's an absolute fraud!"

"You're all frauds. You'd better get to the cemetery."

Volushka left them, running as fast as he could, all the while doing his best to find his way through the squints of his swollen eyes, pausing every twenty yards to catch his breath or rub the stitch in the side of his enormous, injured body. Running in half-blinded circles through the streets or doubled over wheezing and gasping in pain, the villagers jeered at him for what they thought was a typical drunken display, if they even cared at all what it was or wasn't. By the time he came to the bottom of the cemetery hill, he was crawling on his hands and knees.

"Hold it! Everyone, wait! Everyone, just wait!"

He turned over on his back exhausted and just lay there like a palpitating lump. The villagers at the top of the hill cat-called him, laughing and aping him with unconfined jollity; even the little soi-disant corpse grinned. The Undertaker, who kept his own deliberate pace to avoid both the association with him and Volushka's smell, passed him to go up the hill, shaking his head.

The villagers then threw rocks at him in their disgusted impatience.

After getting hit in the face, Volushka staggered to his feet and stumbled in little zigzags up the hill. As he finally crested and caught up even with them, he was still being hit with stones.

"Listen! Ok! That's enough!"

"Well, *you* seem to have come to the right place, I think there's another open grave over there," Marcabrusa said with a lift in his eternally sunny personality.

Volushka grabbed at Marcabrusa's general direction, the blood running afresh down his face and his eyes swollen and throbbing but grabbed Mrs. Julka and shook her violently.

"It's your fault! You're the pestilential reason that this beautiful little girl is here! I told everyone! This is the man that's brought it all to your door!"

Mrs. Julka slapped him in the head repeatedly and all the villagers kicked him until he let her go.

"Volushka couldn't be more wrong, though I understand the easy suspicion," Marcabrusa said solemnly. "My friends, I haven't run away, and I have nothing to hide. You can do what you want with me but I'm here til the end to help. I am happy to be attached to the family, to pray with them and work for them in this difficult time, I'll do whatever the village needs...

"I know this man is your Grave Listener and one of your own, a man you all trust, but for his benefit and yours, considering the awful condition he's in, I want to offer again my services to keep vigil for the girl, to listen for her, and I will remain steadfast in this cemetery for as many days and nights as you wish. I'll do so for your peace of mind and my honor alone, no pay, only a little food to keep my strength for her."

"This man is a fraud, he's not a Grave Listener! He needs to be arrested! Are you going to leave the fate of this girl in this stranger's hands, the very stranger who did this to her, a conniving and a smooth gyrovague who will take on any guise to defraud you, assume any profession to beguile you into his traps?! Now he's a Grave Listener? A man without methods, who you know nothing about? This is the soigné Incubus you want to send into the darkness with this little girl?"

The villagers looked each man over silently, slowly and with burning suspicion. Before Marcabrusa could speak, the Undertaker stepped forward.

"I don't like either of these men and I don't trust them, not at all. I personally think we'd be better off without both of them, and I wonder what we're building a brand-new Gallows for if not for the likes of these. I don't like this Grave Listening business, I think its sacrilegious, disrespectful to the dead and an unnecessary prolonging of grief. But if you're set on hoping for this girl, I think we should rely on this disgusting idiot who we know was born for this filthy thing."

"And what should we do with Marcabrusa?" one of the villagers asked.

"Have him finish the Gallows and then hang him on it!" Volushka snapped. "You'll put an end to this plague before it gets started!"

"I would even be glad to help you with your Gallows. But this isn't the plague I have seen," Marcabrusa said. "There are no black rupturing boils, there's no madness, no sweating fevers, just a peaceful disappearance into sleep and a ghostly purple pallor. It is startling in its calm. This hasn't come in with me and I am as suspicious and frightened as you are. There must be strange powers in the air, some awful influence in our midst. And without a priest, the whole village is unprotected and at the mercy of diabolical forces. But I am resolved to stand with you to confront them, even if I may ultimately succumb to them. The little girl is the most important thing now, tell me what you want me to do."

The villagers looked at each other pleased, which made Volushka look up to Heaven in audible disbelief. They shouted at him for interrupting their admiration, grabbed him and pushed him toward the open grave.

"We'd better not catch you loafing around or drunk or ran away or so help you, God, we'll rip out your living guts."

"When have I ever? I'm an absolute professional! I'm your best hope when you're on the other end! Only, I don't have all my equipment."

"Why not this time, you idiot?"

"You people threw it all over the street."

"Well, you better go down and get it, and fast."

Some of the big villagers chased him down the hill and out of the gate.

Volushka wandered around the street sadly, looking for all his tools. Belka's dog, always running around, barked incessantly as he shadowed him. His whole body ached, and he wished he could go to the brothel and lay down in the fluffy beds with Magaden or Luba or even Beskovina. He thought about running away but knew he was not as handsome or dynamic as Marcabrusa and that, even if he were, you were not safe as a stranger in a village; Marcabrusa himself will soon be building his own Gallows, and the thought cheered him for a moment. He picked up and put on his battered *Uphegia* garland, found most of his tubes, his mallet, two bulbs of garlic. He crawled under the steps of the tavern to get his stop plate. He couldn't find his flasks.

He stood in the middle of the street lost in his sadness and imagination. He was sad that he was alone and yet desperate to be left alone. He felt as alone as the sun that stood there like him, walking its sad, setting steps toward the cemetery on the hill. And he mourned for the whole world that was only this street and this cemetery. He thought of all the fanciful places he always lied about and wished he had actually lived in one of them. When he turned from the sun to return to the cemetery, Benzi was there behind him with the crushed Victrola horn. Benzi gave him the horn and then, without saying anything, he and Bunny left him there in the street.

The Blacksmith nailed the stop plate to the coffin and Volushka put the tubes he could find into the plate. The villagers and Marcabrusa buried the girl and left Volushka to listen. He watched them disappear down the hill and from his vantage could see them in the distance walking to the tavern.

They left him no food or blossom wine and without his flasks, Volushka only had his wits and his personal character, such as it was, to see him through the nights of Witches and vampires and ghosts. But it was especially important that he do this job right, for the dignity of all Grave Listeners in his life-and-death rivalry with this interloper, with all his wickedness and charm. He resolved to be sober and serious in his duty, to be upright and courageous, as an advocate for the little girl and against all the powers of darkness that threatened her. He would be a saving angel to the frightened daughter imprisoned underground and only take naps when absolutely necessary.

After being beaten up all day, and with devastating injuries all over his body, he thought it best to start with a nap. Even the softest breeze agonized him as it brushed his swollen face and he knew he had to be top fit if he was to overcome all the adversaries that marshalled against him. A short, powerful nap would restore him to his fighting glory and then he would dedicate himself absolutely and completely to his sacred charge.

He slept for almost a full day. At first, because the afternoon light appeared unchanged and the lonely sexton was ringing the Church bell again, he thought he had slept for a mere twenty minutes but he realized, to his horror, that his dereliction was complete and discovered: there were two bowls at his feet, one empty and one with a chipmunk greedily eating his food. A third bowl of slumgullion was poured all over him, which must have been why he dreamed a prostitute fed him sloppy from a small, golden bowl.

If this was reported back to the villagers, they would surely be back in force to beat him to death or worse, bury him alive. For all he knew, they were on their way now and so he scrambled to collect his things, swatted away the chipmunk and gulped down what was left. He started to run away, perhaps to the neighboring village of the poisonous marshes where he would take his chances reinventing himself as a man of composite virtues.

But as he took his first stumbling steps, he thought he heard a noise come from the tube in the ground.

He put the horn back on the tube and listened — was it a cry? He called into the horn.

"Hello? It's Volushka, can you hear me? Hello? If you cannot speak, can you move? Can you knock on the coffin?"

He couldn't hear a voice — but could he hear breathing?

"Malva, if you're alive and can hear me, can you make any noise at all?" ...Nothing — and then, a rustle!

"Hold on little girl, I will get the villagers! Don't worry, we'll have you out soon! Just relax and breathe slowly! Hold on, Malva Makovöd!"

Volushka ran down the hill as fast as he could until, toward the bottom of the hill, he stumbled in his excitement and smacked his head on a headstone. He leapt directly to his feet, cursing, and sped off in a waddle toward the tavern, crying out again and again in the street as he went.

"Help! Everyone! Come out! It's Malva! She's alive! Come out and help!"

He burst into the tavern. It was crowded again, as expected with Marcabrusa now holding court. The villagers started on him right away.

"What the Hell are you doing down here, you damned piece of —"

"Shut up and listen! Just shut up! It's Malva Makovöd, she's alive! Everyone come to the cemetery and bring your shovels! She's alive!"

Everyone ran into the street and up the hill of the cemetery, rejoicing as they went. Volushka, by this point, was absolutely winded and lagged behind with the older women, pulling up at intervals to catch his breath and rub the pain in his side. The old women finally left him behind, shaking their head in disgust. When he finally crested the hill, he saw the villagers hard at work together, digging as fast as they could, working quickly down to the coffin. The villagers who were not working surrounded the grave in a large circle, cheering on the diggers and chattering expectantly. Volushka could not see a way inside the circle and, though no less excited, resigned himself to lingering at the back.

When he heard the collective gasp from the crowd, and then their screams and wailing, he started running.

The women cried for the dead child. Some fainted when they saw the blood at the corner of her lips and the bugs crawling over her once innocent face. The villagers searched the group for Volushka and when they turned to see him fleeing the cemetery, they chased him with a murderous vengeance.

Benzi had been playing in the street with one of the village dogs when he saw Volushka approaching in another one of his spastic escapes, his horn and tools flying off his body in the street. The dog started barking at Volushka and other dogs, excited by the chase and the shouting, joined the mob running behind. Benzi called to Volushka as he approached.

"Are you getting killed?"

"Get out of here! It's bad! Get out of my way!"

When Volushka caught up even with him, he stumbled over the dog, who yelped and then started chasing him, nipping at his legs. Benzi and Bunny ran with Volushka, too.

"If you're not going to run faster than this you should probably just kill yourself!"

"Go home! I mean it, get out of here! I can't be watching out for you, they're going to tear me to pieces!"

"I know, it's going to be awful!"

"Get this damn dog off of me!"

"His name's Cookies!"

"I don't care what his damned name is! Go take him someplace!"

"He's not my dog, he's just a friend of mine."

"O my God, I don't think I'm going to make it!"

"If you're going to explode, don't get it on me!"

"Quick, for God's sakes, go into the *Uphegia*!"

They made it into the fields with the crowd nearly on them. They ran together, darting and zigzagging in, out and around the maze of tall stalks and broad leaves with the angry villagers pursuing them into the shadows, throwing rocks at Volushka (or where they thought Volushka was) in their confusion and wrath. Everyone was running in all directions, crashing into each other and smashing into the *Uphegia* plants, releasing into the air all their little white flowers that then circled and danced in the breezes and fluttered over everyone like snow. The screaming, the cursing and the barking dogs rumbled the fields until the whole dark forest became a roaring, infernal garden of horror and malice and sorrow. In the dark under the tall plants and the enormous leaves, with the little white flowers flying everywhere, villagers were injuring themselves with rocks and punches, tearing up the fields in their fury, dissolving into cyclones of lunacy and self-eating violence. Benzi was laughing as he and Volushka ran in circles around the maze, Cookies was jumping all over Benzi to play and Volushka was bleeding down the side of his face from one of the rocks. When the villagers could not catch Volushka, they finally petered out to a stop and left the fields, spent and injured, vowing to do terrible things when they found him. Meanwhile, Volushka and Benzi ran all the way to the back of the fields and out through the circle of the woods into a bright and bristling meadow.

They had somehow survived and in their incredulous ecstasy, they laughed and danced together, rejoicing in the snowfall of little white flowers flying all around them, leaping to catch them or pointing and giggling at each other as the flowers landed like crowns of frost in their hair. They regaled each other with tales of their personal bravery or agility, the narrow escapes from certain capture and the time they crashed through a group of old women who, facing the other way, had no idea what hit them, squawking as they hit the ground. Volushka swept Benzi into his arms and they blundered through a made-up tune, spinning around in the flying white flowers when suddenly, Cookies started whimpering and then ran away through the forest.

Volushka froze.

Ahead of him stood a figure in black robes, in long black gloves covering its claws and a towering, black triangular hood that masked the creature's face. On its left arm hung a basket full of simples.

It stared quietly at the two of them.

"Who's that?"

"Don't look at it. Hold on to your Bunny."

Volushka shielded Benzi by cuddling him close in his arms, holding his head to prevent him from turning to look and he backed away slowly into the forest as the figure watched them go.

5 RIVALS FOR THE LAND OF THE DEAD

"Everyone still wants to kill you."

"Well, I still want to kill all of them! Where is everybody?"

"At the cemetery again. They're digging up Druka, Marcabrusa saved her, too."

Volushka crept out cautiously from the *Uphegia* where he'd been hiding for the last three weeks, emerging each day to see if the mood in the village improved. It hadn't. He leapt down the little slope and sat again on the log with Benzi and Bunny.

"He's not saving them, he's the one putting them in the ground! This whole plague started on his arrival! What he's doing up there is a sin!"

"He's just listening and telling everyone."

"It's not just listening, he's not credentialed! It's completely outside the fraternity, the natural order! He doesn't have the Seals, he doesn't have the birthright and he doesn't have the craft! He's going to mess the whole thing up and then he'll be in trouble for sure!"

"Like you?"

"Something demonic and strange must have happened, she was laughing and farting when I left her! I wouldn't put it past Marcabrusa to have sent a spell to murder her right where she lived, in league with his many wicked shadows! How else are you going to explain what's happening? You think people just wake up out of their graves all the time? How does he keep finding them alive if he's not putting them there in the first place?"

"He's using your tools. He wears the horn on his head, too, but he's not as disgusting. He's making all sorts of money and friends and maybe everybody loves him."

"That son of a bitch! I'll kill him, God help me! I'll murder him! It's a criminal fraud, I want him hanged up! I'm going to the Church, I want justice!"

"My Aunt said they wrote to the Bishop for a new priest but because we're cursed, they haven't sent anyone or wrote back. Why don't you just beat him up? Didn't you beat up a hundred guys and a Principessa?"

"I didn't beat up a Principessa, you idiot! I was in a furious combat and, you know what, I'm not explaining this to you since you're just going to be a fatal pain in the ass about it! I don't have enough on my shoulders right now, hiding in the woods and eating slugs to survive, I need to have you work me into the grave!"

"Because you can't beat up a Principessa."

"I can beat up twenty Principessas!"

"So, what was so tough about this one? Was she some kind of imbecile wolfman?"

"Principessas aren't imbecile wolfmen, she was a goddess of beauty who fell madly in love with me but was betrothed to a cousin as part of a complicated land deal! It's the nobility, not something I can explain to a five-year-old!"

"If this imbecile wolfman loved you, it seems like she was also blind and had no sense of smell, so how she was able to beat you up is confusing."

"She didn't beat me up, stop inventing things, you wicked little brat! You're absolutely wicked! Get thee behind me, Satan!"

"That'll take all day!"

"You son of a bitch, how would you like to tangle right now?!"

"How would *you* like to tangle right now?"

"You want to see me beat up a Principessa, just try throwing some fists at me!"

"I'm going to punch you a million miles away!"

"Go ahead and try, you little brat!"

Benzi leaped on his back and Volushka jumped around like an angry horse until Benzi's little laughter circled around and around them as they played.

"Don't step on Bunny!"

Volushka bent down to pick up the rabbit and they all galloped around the log until another shadow joined them, and the romping stopped.

"I thought I heard the three-headed monster that's causing this awful plague," said Marcabrusa, standing above them at the top of the little slope with a warm and pleasant smile.

Volushka was so incensed, he forgot to put Benzi down.

"You stupid asshole, I'm going to kill you right now! You've got some crust coming down here, I want my tools back!"

"Well, you didn't seem to be using them and there's been a lot of trouble lately, so I just thought I'd help a little to try and get things under control. Some of these things I just found lying in the street so I figured you wouldn't mind."

"I damn well mind! Those tools are sacred to the trade and not to be profaned by just any conniving asshole who wants to play at a mortal business! And don't think I don't

43

know who the cause of this plague is! Once I snap your damned neck, the plague will be lifted, and the villagers will see the real criminal behind it all!"

"And you'll be able to stop eating slugs!" Benzi said, and Volushka put him and Bunny down on the log.

"You seem upset, and I'd recommend a change in diet if you want to get your cheerful outlook back. And far from profaning anything, it seems like everything has been going really well, we already saved nine people in the last few weeks, with Druka being the latest grateful recovery. Now, if you feel some injustice has occurred, I'm glad to go with you to speak to the villagers and step aside if they request it. They seem like a reasonable people, and there has already been so much heartache and conflict, I'm sure we can come to a fair and sober resolution to this whole unfortunate situation."

"You'd love that, you son of a bitch, you turned my own people against me!"

"That's a little unfair, and I don't mean to give offense, but you didn't seem very popular from the start."

"What the Hell would you know about it? You come here smooth as a serpent, you flutter your eyes and ensorcell everyone and now they all want to kill me!"

"I have no idea how you and I became such fast adversaries, believe me. I've been nothing if not warm and polite since we first met in the cemetery, and there were a few times that I tried to defend you when the villagers were saying all sorts of nasty things about you, as much as I could. It's heartbreaking to me, really. Is there a reason why we should be such enemies? Why not work together? It seems lately that there's enough work for both of us and if I know plagues, there's sure to be a lot more. You could be my assistant."

"Your assist— You asshole! You take that horn off right now or I'll take your head right off your neck!!"

"Now, that's pretty ungrateful considering your current community standing. As your manager, I'd have to recommend that you ease your way back in."

Volushka was nonplussed. Benzi cuddled Bunny and yawned.

"That's good advice to you, sir. The only other course that I can see is one where you leave the village. I, of all people, know it can be done so you shouldn't have a single reservation about it, I'm speaking from experience. It's easy and you get a fresh start. A handsome fellow like you, if you can stop shitting on yourself and wear something over your face, should have no problem charming any friendly village you find and you can take any job you want."

Volushka rushed up the slope and tried tackling Marcabrusa, but the awkward upward angle of attack caused him to stumble at the top and he fell in a lump at Marcabrusa's feet. Marcabrusa waited for him to get up, shaking his head as he rolled onto his back and then tried desperately to sit up. He finally managed to stand and picked up his pants as he caught his breath.

Marcabrusa then punched him in the face.

Volushka's head snapped back and it returned slowly into place with a stupefied expression and only half its memories. When he recovered enough to realize that he was just punched in the face, he lunged at Marcabrusa and the two grappled furiously, Volushka's size finally aiding him. They wrestled and they strangled each other, they gouged each other's eyes, they struck at each other with quick, close-quarter blows. They rolled around and around in an angry ball until Volushka pulled Marcabrusa's beautiful hair, he responded by twisting Volushka's genitals, Volushka then bit him. They finally tumbled down the slope and came to a crashing stop against the log, with Marcabrusa straddling on top and holding a knife to Volushka's neck.

"I want you to listen to me very carefully. I'm not going to kill you because I know the boy loves you. But if we meet again, I won't be kind, I won't spare you and as a solemn promise, I'll make it hurt." He stuck the knife up Volushka's nose. "Go anywhere else. It's my hill. It's my cemetery. It's my horn and hat."

He slowly got off Volushka and backed up the slope with the knife out. He picked up the tools from where they were strewn, put the horn on his head, tipped his hat and left.

"Is there a reason why you can't beat anybody up?"

"I had him! I was right on top of him when he played it dirty, some sort of cowardly Trojan move! You don't see that with respectable men! If the ground up there wasn't so damned soft, I would have had him pinned and then would have torn his lungs right out of his face! Let's see how lucky he gets next time!"

"The ground always seems to be soft when you're on it."

"This village must have been built directly over Hell! Dammit, I think I hurt my back…"

"Well, if laying on top of him didn't work, I don't know what else will. You looked like a bag of potatoes!"

"Don't aggravate me because I'm coiled to strike! Besides, I have to think of my next move, I can't go back and forth with you about who looks like what! Why don't you go home and bring back some food?"

"I'm not hungry."

"Not for you, for me!"

"I don't have any slugs at home! I'm not a slob!"

"You get over here so I can wring your neck!"

"You get over here so I can wring *your* neck!"

"You don't have any slugs at home, how would you like a slug in the head?"

"How would you like a rhinoceros in your head?"

"That's just stupid, what do you know about rhinoceroses?"

"My Uncle told me a story."

"That genius. Everyone's got an idiot Uncle! Didn't your Uncle get his testicles caught in a butter churn?"

"Didn't you get your face caught in a stupid churn?"

"You're Uncle's real smart, all right. When has he ever seen a rhinoceros?"

"He's only seen the back of one..."

"Don't even say it…"

"…When you show up."

"You little runt! Come over here so I can strangle you!"

"With what, your odor?"

"You stupid pain in the ass, you got some awful sass!"

"You're the one that's stupid!"

"I'm the only one who knows anything in this village!"

"My Uncle knows more than you, he tells me lots of stories!"

"Like what?"

"About animals and the stars and ghosts and Witches."

"Ghosts and Witches aren't stories. They're real and I've seen them."

"And they have magic."

"That's right. Many's the night I kept vigil in the graveyard and encountered a terrible ghost hungering for human flesh. It's all I could do to fight them off. Vampires and Witches, with mysterious powers beyond our understanding, driven by malice to work our ruin. There's not a man, or a troop of men, that can gainstand their magic, animal strength and wickedness."

"Marcabrusa can."

"He could not! That's ridiculous! He'd be torn limb from limb and then devoured! Where would you get that idea? Or are you just aggravating the shit out of me again?!"

"You said you fought off terrible ghosts and Marcabrusa just threw *you* all around! So, that means he could beat up a whole bunch of ghosts and Witches!"

"He didn't throw me all around, I slipped on the ground!"

"You slipped on the ground as he was throwing you."

"He wasn't throwing me! I got undermined by the landscape! Nobody can beat up Witches, especially that lucky fopdoodle!"

"So how come you were able to?"

"I knew the arcane tricks and even then, I barely got out alive! Descending from generations of Grave Listeners has given me a survival edge, don't make the mistake to think that anybody can just beat up vampires and Witches! That's the fastest way to get killed!"

"So why don't you just go up to the cemetery tonight, wait for a Witch and say, 'Can you eat Marcabrusa for me?' And if she says, 'No, I want to eat *you*!' you can sashay around like beef to distract her, then use your arcane tricks to trap her and make her under your powers?"

"Does everything you say have to be stupid and annoying? Making deals with Witches can only lead to damnation and disasters, they have powers you cannot even imagine! Especially your little five-year-old jellied brain! You've never even seen a Witch!"

"Yes, I have!"

"No, you haven't! When?"

"The other day! You weren't there, you were eating slugs."

"If you had seen a Witch, you'd already be boiled down into a disgusting potion! Stop talking about things you don't know anything about!"

"I would just punch her in the nose and she would be knocked out!"

"You'd better not let a Witch hear you talking like that! They are a wicked presence everywhere, can hear across vast provinces and strike you down from a terrible height and distance! They lurk in every tree, under every mushroom, in all the shadows. Even now, a Witch may be plotting to get you!"

"Well, if you're afraid of Witches, I guess you'll just have to keep slipping on the ground and having a knife shoved up your nose."

"I'm not afraid of Witches!"

"I meant if you're terrified of Witches."

"I'm not afraid of Witches! And besides, I'm not going to slip the next time! Next time, I'm going to be sticking *my foot* up his nose!"

Benzi and Bunny looked at him with little faces wrinkled with doubts. As Volushka waited for another smart remark, he started getting more and more annoyed in the silence.

Aggravation swarmed in his head. *I'm not afraid of Witches,* Volushka thought, *and if I was, it would only be sensible, knowing the savagery of Hell and besides, I don't need to consult dark powers at the peril of my soul to thrash an imbecile like Marcabrusa, who was only minutes away from being torn to shreds if I hadn't lost my base, I have half a mind to walk straight into the village and pull his scrawny ass out of that damned tavern and beat him to death in front of all his friends, who I hasten to add are just as guilty for the plague by abetting this criminal, and drinking and eating with him; maybe he needs Witches and special devils to be brave and patently* delightful but no one needs any supernatural explanations for my virtues — though if I _did_ enter into an infernal compact to rid this village of all its scum, God would probably appreciate my derring-do, my zeal for justice, and lay out a celebratory banquet the likes of which that poky, rat-infested tavern could only dream of, while also consigning those imbeciles to eating slugs for eternity as they are getting bent and sodomized, all the while begging me for one bite of my partridge and grapes, my peacock and ambrosia and now, God dammit, I want lunch, the right lunch, with a wedge of cake and some pudding like a decent man deserves! You know, I'm getting pretty tired grazing like an animal and eating leeches and slugs while that idiot is being served pheasant and sherbet by his demonic footmen, and I guess the more I really think about Election, fairness and the balance of it all, including, but not limited to, lunch, the more I think the only _expeditious_ solution involves Witches; I'm not afraid of Witches as much as I respect their powers and I certainly have all the vocational tools and experience to defend myself from the snares of Hell, moreso than any other man, and I also have Righteousness on my side! And as it's obvious that he is supported by demons, it's only logical to combat Marcabrusa's unnatural wickedness with my own. If by their aid, he's the superior man, it only makes sense to employ supernatural agencies to balance the odds; if I'm the superior man, my demons would be nothing more than accessories to the inevitable result. I mean, on consideration, it couldn't be more clear. Or am I an animal constrained by villains to repast on bran bugs? No, I am a man fated to complete a noble and sacred mission! To confront a Witch and overcome, this is the stuff that troubadours celebrate and Ladies swoon over! …I wonder if the brothel will let a hero in to get a last grab in case I'm eaten by the Witch or else dragged into the bowels of Hell, or maybe I better not, don't want to lose focus or face a Witch with the

logy and slackness that comes after a powerful round of lovemaking,
although if we're being honest with ourselves, we can note here without
any false modesty that we have the deep reserves of strength and
stamina of ten lovemaking men and so shouldn't therefore be worried
at all by getting in a light amorous interlude if it doesn't include
acrobatics, aquatics or complicated rope play and a long idea
entranced him, out of the wind, from under the
mushrooms and out of the shadows, out of the mystery of
the air, an elaborate and fantastical plan, too bold and
complex for lesser men but now entrusted to him with its
own righteous and terrible instancy. He smiled at his own
breathtaking ingenuity and he drifted away for some time
turning it over in his mind. Benzi giggled quietly watching
the dumb expression of awe from which Volushka never
recovered as he strode away with martial confidence and a
gleam in his wicked eyes.

Nobody can beat up Witches.

6 THE WITCH OF GORE MAL GORE

Volushka marched up the little slip and through the *Uphegia* toward the meadow beyond the surrounding forest. He imagined the tall plants were giants, trembling before him as they swayed softly in the breeze, while in his head trumpets made a heroic fanfare. He reveled in his cunning, the plan to put Marcabrusa under his heel, and savored in the rejoicing the villagers would lavish on him after they were freed from the plague. He could see his enemies put to flight and a new place of honor within the village; he could have his pick at the brothel, no more having his genitals mangled by that awful Rutchka! And instead of the carping of the awful hags always shitting on him, he could now hear the voices of his ancestors praising him, the culmination of a great destiny and a noble line. He was brave, and strong and a man of spectacular promise!

"How many asses do you actually have?"

Volushka turned around in a startled fury to see Benzi behind him.

"Counting you, two!"

"No wonder you sleep all day, I'd be tired, too, if I had to drag that all around."

"Go home! I don't have the time to be put through it by you right now!"

"Why, are you going to cry?"

"What? No, I'm not going to cry…"

"It's ok to cry if you're fat and stupid."

"I'M NOT GOING TO CRY! I'm going to do something very important and dangerous!"

"You're going to take a shit?"

"NO!! You brat!.... You…" Volushka looked around to see if anyone was listening. "Can you keep a secret?"

"No."

Volushka nearly chewed through his tongue in his frustration, biting back the urge to kill him. When he recovered, he kneeled down to speak face to face with Benzi, with a solemn purpose and a secret, serious voice. Benzi drew in close with awe to listen.

"…I'm going to visit the Witch of Gore Mal Gore."

"Whoa!..."

"The Witch of Gore Mal Gore is the most evil creature you would ever have the terrible misfortune to meet, in league with the very Devil himself! Many a stout man, the very bravest Knights, have never returned from her lair. They say the bottom of her body is nothing but a coiled serpent's tail on which she sits, a once famous beauty made hideous and deformed by her foul lusts and schemes. She controls the lightning, spreads discord and plagues, causes frogs and vermin to overrun kingdoms. She turned the battle against Faldobar at Regosparta when he refused to pay homage to her. Her face is just a mouth of fangs, and her breath can melt iron and spoil gold! And she especially hates little boys, killing them and eating their bones, while boiling down their fat to make her poisonous malefactions!"

"O my God, can I come?!"

"What??! No, you can't come!"

"Please!!"

"What— No! Were you even listening?! For Christ's sakes! It's like… WHAT'S WRONG WITH YOU?!"

"Ok, bring me back something!" he said, running away with Bunny.

"I can't… it's not a…….. shop…"

Volushka stomped off through the forest aggravated.

The meadow bloomed in anticipation of his arrival. Its perfume led him away from the village, down a violet path and through a long, wicked allée farther and farther away from the sunlight until he came to a flowering bog, edged with gold and black thistles, and surrounded by The Very Human Vultures. A little stone path rose out of the bog and led him to a dark, ramshackle hut.

A putrid smoke hissed out from the door in slinky ophidian coils while the ravenous little peony patch in the dooryard was littered with the bones of mice, frogs, voles, and morons. The bog bubbled behind him, and the dark pressed him forward with its menacing voices of temptation, flattery, and promise. The Very Human Vultures followed and alighted on the roof and over the door. Inside, a last pocket of breath from a small child disappeared into a boil of water.

Volushka desperately wanted to leave but the path closed behind him in a wall of brambles and voices, festooned with angry beehives, slithering monsters and venomous creepers; a fluffle of black rabbits piled in a strange little menace at the base of the wall. Frozen where he stood, he felt his belly being pulled through the door.

The smoke and the smell disoriented him, and the dark was oppressive. He stumbled into the hut and instantly crashed into a small butcher's table from which enormous rats and giant vinegaroons scattered, while jars of powders and oils rolled off the table and around his feet. His eyes watered and he could not adjust to the dark as he felt for the wall, backing himself against it to prevent the phantasmagoria from sneaking up from behind.

The form of a body slowly emerged from a flickering mist, surrounded by a poisonous corona. A croaking, ancient, hollow voice pulled itself out of a raspy echo and shivered in its loneliness, wroth and infernal grief.

"You're a plump one."

The Witch gathered the last of the mist into her form and stood before Volushka. Her body was young and fresh and beautiful, lovely in its curves which flowed like milk into sleek legs that stood on delicate bare feet. Her breasts were enormous, spilling out of her graveclothes, split down the center in its impossible décolletage, so heavy that Atlas himself could not support them. She was merely an accessory to them, and she reveled in their lascivious power.

And yet, her arms and neck were gray, green, black and decaying, covered in bugs, and her hands finished at long fingers tipped with awful claws. The putrefaction crowned her head where her hair had been burned away and appeared only in tight patches of red, filthy straw. The hair on her chin was like the legs of a centipede and her face was covered by a crude mask childishly drawn that barely veiled a horrible, skeletal face, the empty eye sockets just peering over the top of the mask.

Volushka was at once urgently aroused and fearfully repulsed by her Eros and Thanatos and he stumbled around in his confusion, knocking into the walls in his erotic horror.

"I am sorry to disturb you, and for the mess, I tripped over the flowers by the door. I have not come here to do you harm, I have come, Good Lady, to seek your help."

"Thank goodness, how I feared for my life."

"No, Good Lady, I am a man of honor, a respecter of women. I am here on an important quest to rid my village of a pernicious plague and evil."

"A plague and a rival."

"He's a usurper and a seducer! First, he turned the villagers against me, now he's Grave Listening in my place!"

"He sounds daring."

"I'm daring, he's an idiot!"

"You poor thing. And you're unable to vanquish an idiot?"

"I can squash him at a swat! It's the whole village, that's the problem!"

"Idiots make kingdoms. You'll need something broad and fitting. I can make you King of the Fleas."

"I was thinking something a little grander."

"Do not vilipend the little things. A command of fleas can drive a people insane, fearfully, stupidly and murderously. I see you are already acquainted."

"I don't want to destroy everybody, just him. And I want my place back! But with a little more shine on it."

"Just a little?"

"I thought, Good Lady, you would know it best and therefore how best to achieve it. I have money."

"Money."

"Yes, and I can get more once I can get back to the graves."

"What would I do with money?"

"Well, I am not going to sell my soul or enter into a bargain with your Master."

"I don't think my Master is too concerned about it."

"Then what do you want?"

"Warmth."

"It seems infernal enough in here as it is."

She floated toward him and also magically appeared behind him, running her claws through his hair and along his neck.

"How cherubically stupid. I like it when my little chubby ones are dull, they're much easier to subdue and eat." She pinched his belly.

Volushka tried to separate himself but she coiled and tangled around him, becoming a mist in those parts where he tried to grab her or push. She finally waved her hand and threw him to the floor.

"You disgusting things come here in your arrogance solely to demand of me, some potion or spell or service, to commit wicked deeds to slake your deviant little thirsts and then run away to enjoy your perverse delights, while I am regarded as some wicked monster and outcast to the bogs. And you think your money or your soul or some other pointless thing is enough to dazzle and buy me, as if I were one of you and not your serpent. Who has come here for something as simple as a cup of tea? Or to bring some flowers? Instead, my curse is to create your love charms so you can slither away and live out your happy little lives, even as I feel your terrible bliss in my heart. I have destroyed so many for that arrogance and their presumption, I should be cold and vengeful to you, too, for your stupidity and pride. Instead, I have come out of the dark, the mist and the centuries to entreat you, to ask for contact and for touch. What you desire, I can give you. What I desire is the same human price."

The Witch waved at the darkened back of the room and two torches blazed to life over a magically sumptuous bed.

"You want me to love you?"

"As if you could. And I could easily enslave you, as I have done to many men and women, and eat you when you cloy and no longer please me. But I am so tired. And I have no illusions. I simply want a moment that is human again, connected and engaged and warm, if only a moment."

"With me?"

"Yes, with an idiot like you."

"I don't know if I can."

"Are you not a man that has the deep reserves of strength and stamina of ten lovemaking men?"

"I wouldn't want to overstate it..."

"Does my body not please you?"

"Yes, it is beautiful, in its connubial parts, but your... I mean, when it comes to kissing, well, there's the mask..."

"Would you like me to remove it?"

"NO! No. It's difficult. I respond to a certain earthy look. Are you able to complete the illusion?"

"No."

"There's a lot to consider here between us, morally and spiritually, I would feel terrible if I broke your heart, I also hurt my back when I fell on some soft ground, I should probably return when I can provide the performance you richly deserve, and then there's the question of being eaten or boiled afterward, which tends to thwart my sexual aptitude..."

"If you leave, you will surely be destroyed by your rival. I can give you the power to best him and take your place at the head of your village, respected in your trade, with a new ability to commune with the dead but you will have to hold me, to please me, to give me anything human in return."

"How?"

She conjured in her hands a fat, black pouch.

"This powerful charm, this sprinkle of black powder, can mimic death for a time, masking the heartbeat and making the breath imperceptible, even creating a pallor and a stink. A Grave Listener, a cunning one, who wanted to show the people a waking corpse, could certainly devise a little plan."

"It looks like the powder of a ground up Night Gruesome."

"It has some of that flower in it, and it resembles the dying from it. But you don't wake from eating a Night Gruesome alone."

"Those torches are bright."

"Yes."

"I don't know if we'd prefer the ambiance of a dark and smoky room…"

"I want to look into your eyes."

"Ok… Because of my back, I might need a little help."

"Drink this."

"O God, what's in this?"

"This and That."

"This won't make me hideous or deranged, will it? I'm doing this in good faith."

"Drink it."

Volushka drank the concoction and choked on it for several minutes as the Witch waited silently. His eyes watered uncontrollably as she led him to the bed, and the heat prickled in his loins.

He now had the power of ten lovemaking men and was flustered and miserable. Her body was a soft, paradisal delight and he pawed over her enormous breasts, thrilling to her curves, the giving bounty, the glory that rose to meet him with such gigantic and supple desires. Her body was a contact of silk, so warm, so famished and therefore so spirited, it was love, it felt like love, and she enfolded him, he thrilled in his belly with the cool, smooth shocks of skin to soft skin.

Down his back she ran her awful claws and then she grabbed him by his throat. She groaned with old, sick groans, wheezing, and her mask, which threatened to tear away, smeared its face under his sweat into a grotesque sorrow. Her green and gray decay stank, and her breath was cadaverine. He worked harder and faster to try and finish as she drove her claws into his neck and the hair on her chin wiggled its legs. He now heard behind him the Vultures in the room, and the pot began to boil, the shadow curled in circles around the ceiling. They rose together to a climax as the rats and vinegaroons ran across the floor and up into the bed, and she began laughing until it sounded to him like she was crying, and Volushka was frightened. But under the power of her potion, they both finally released with towering ecstasy; and as he climaxed, a big, awful spider crawled out of her eye socket and raised its long black legs as it sat on the scribble of her mask.

Volushka ran down the path toward the bog and when he felt far enough away to be safe, he stopped and vomited something black and hairy, and the vomit ran away. The thorny obstacles parted and the path opened into the moonlight. He doubled over gasping with pain in his belly but finally looked with devious pride at the powder he had earned in his big, grubby hands. Volushka now had the charm to bury who he wished and be there when they woke, the savior of the villagers. And in the end, he would poison Marcabrusa and be there to hear his waking terror in his coffin and leave him there buried alive.

He rejoiced in his plan and power, he marveled and laughed at overcoming the Witch, he gazed up at the night sky with the calm, settled comfort of one who has come through a terrible trial.

He started to walk triumphantly back to the village when all of a sudden his heart sank, and he became sick. Panicked and morose, he looked at the stars and cursed himself.

He ran back to the Witch.

Before he could enter the hut, her hand emerged from the door, palm up and empty, stopping him in his tracks.

She closed her hand and opened it, revealing now a little skull with long black hair.

"For the boy."

Volushka grabbed the skull and ran as fast as he could down the path.

The hand disappeared into the hut with the sad whisper of good-bye.

7 A NIGHT AT THE BROTHEL

Volushka returned to the village in the dead of night and lurked between the buildings to remain unseen. He was excited about the prospect of using the Witch's powder, and putting his plan into action, but he would have to avoid getting disemboweled by the villagers to do so. For all that horrible intercourse, he wished he could have also asked for a potion for invisibility and strength. Only the Devil knows though what he would have had to do to secure it. He shivered at the prospect.

Who would be his first victim? Though he would love to unseat Marcabrusa right away and punch all his fawning admirers in their faces, he knew he would have to wait until his standing as a Grave Listener was restored, otherwise he would have to dig him up in order to do so. He *would* somehow have to incapacitate Marcabrusa so he could step up and be the Grave Listener who rescues the various villagers, but he did not relish the idea of a knife up his nose right now. How much powder would it take to just put him to sleep? How would he get him to take it? In his haste to escape the Witch, he never really asked how to use the powder, if there were any precautions to mind, what he could expect in terms of the time between dying and waking. Volushka was certainly not going to go back and ask, that's how little male spiders get eaten.

There was a lot to think about and tying up all the particulars started giving him a headache.

He wondered if they would let him in at the brothel. For all he knew, his headache was Witchery and tragically fatal, as it seemed to come on him supernaturally — and surely even the most cold-hearted prostitute wouldn't deny a dying man one last taste of the persimmon. Magaden was probably not an option and Petchka would certainly kick him in his genitals on sight so sneaking in at the back of the brothel was a sound strategy — perhaps Luba, on an off night and moved by self-sympathy for the woebegone, would take him in her arms, Luba with the pretty little nose and hazel eyes?

Volushka snuck behind the brothel and saw Luba's candlelight in her second-floor bedroom.

He tried climbing the trellis with the idea of swinging over to her window with a nimble flourish but got tangled upside-down halfway up, and in his frantic attempt to free himself from the vines, he broke the trellis in half and crashed to the ground.

He landed on his head and sprained his neck, rolling around in the dark quietly cursing.

He decided instead to throw some small stones at her window to make a sweet petition to her, with the lofty hopes that she would swoon into his arms, as sleek and soft as a melted cheetah.

"Luba, are you awake? Pretty little Luba with the hazel eyes, are you available tonight? I hate to bother you so late, but I think I'm dying, I think I have the frightful stone in my head that's formed from excessive love, I may only have hours to live. Pssst, Luba, are you there, sweet one?"

The candle in the window went out.

"Luba? I have some money and I expect to have a whole lot more, once I get back to the graves, which will be real soon and I promise to lavish you with it. I also promise I'll be quick. Luba?"

The candle in the window was lit again.

"Luba! You won't regret it, I'll soon be a well-respected member of this community, someone you can be proud of, at the head of our council and a genuine leader! Because I am still only potentially respected, could you come downstairs and sneak me in the back door? Luba? Luba, can you hear me? Please come to the window! Help a poor man with a stone!"

The back door of the brothel finally opened and Rutchka emerged, scowling.

"O, for God's sakes! No way! No! There aren't any mentally ill werewolves out here, why don't you go back inside! Where the Hell is Luba?"

Rutchka folded her arms with the same look of disgust she was born with.

"Dammit! All the time! Why, Lord?! O, those thick, God-awful eyebrows! And that breast with its nipple on the side, like a confused squash having a crisis! I think my headache just moved into my balls!"

Rutchka shrugged and started closing the door.

"Ok, wait! Wait! Hold on, Dammit! Wait! …All right, but you better listen to me and stop when I tell you! You're always mangling my testicles!... I need to be discreet, Petchka will do me in if she knows I'm here, can you sneak me inside?"

Rutchka threw her shawl over him and dragged him by his face up the stairs.

When they arrived at the room, Rutchka pushed him toward the bed and because she didn't remove the shawl from over his head, he stumbled and crashed face first into the bed post.

"You stupid idiot! Was that necessary? I'm not going to get enough abuse when you're on top of me destroying my genitals! Let me be on top this time!"

Rutchka looked at him for a minute with her usual nauseous expression and then went behind her privacy screen to wash her underarms.

Volushka bristled with disgust. He rubbed his bloody lip and went to the mirror to check the damage to his face. On the little table, beside the lavender powder, was a bottle of vodka with a glass on top acting like a bottle cap. A devious little smile curled his lips, which hurt.

"Short of blinding ourselves, I think we could both use a strong drink to get through this. Come over here when you're done aggravating your face."

He poured the vodka and sprinkled in a little of the Witch's powder. As he did, he thought about Rutchka's animal strength and the horrifying power of her privates and then sprinkled in a little more.

Rutchka came over, smacked him in the head and took the glass out of his hand. She drank it down and pushed him on the bed. She raised her skirt and got on top of him.

He thought about smothering himself with one of the pillows as she started crushing his groin, bouncing on him from a thrust apex of about two feet, when she suddenly stopped.

Her face, already perpetually twisted into an angry fat, now seemed to turn inside-out and become a ghastly purplish white. She stared into the distance and then closed her eyes peacefully, slumping over his body and smooshing him. Her breast wrapped around his head and the nipple on its side went up his nose on purpose. He struggled to free himself from under her ponderous body and they finally ended up together on the floor.

He scrambled to his feet and stood over her in triumph.

"I've got you! O, I've got you, you poisonous hellcat! Try mashing my balls six feet under! O, you are going to a dark place, a very cold, dark place! But don't be too afraid, No! No! I will come for you, you have the good fortune to be my first, the first step to recovering the graveyard and beating that damned impostor! Though my agonized balls are telling me to count this one as a sample case and leave you buried, poor Rutchka, I'm going to ignore my balls this one time, which is nearly impossible for a man to do. You can thank me when you're pulled out of your wormy grave. But make no mistake, you ox, people around here are going to get what's coming to them, that's for sure!"

Rutchka then opened her eyes.

"Ack! Rutchka, are you ok? Can you hear me? I'll get you a drink, it'll fortify you, try not to move!" He raced for the vodka, powder in hand, when pale Rutchka stood up and started screaming.

Volushka put his hand over her mouth to try and silence her, but she lifted him off the ground and threw him into the wall, screaming louder and more frantically. He put her in a headlock and while trying to pull her head off, she bit him until he let go and then she punched him in the face. She started flailing around the room in uncontrollable spasms, screaming and vomiting and breaking everything, until there was broken glass and furniture everywhere.

Everyone in the brothel was now banging on the door and half the villagers were roused from their houses and queueing excitedly at the back of the brothel below the window.

Volushka was beside himself with terror and cowering under her nightgown in the corner, covered in lavender and broken glass. He saw no way out and, tortured by visions of his prolonged and gruesome death at the hands of the villagers, he cried softly beneath her screaming.

As Volushka was strangling himself with the nightgown, Rutchka suddenly flung herself onto a side table and the candles instantly set her alight, from crown to toe, in an absolutely phantasmagoric ball of fire. She bounced off the walls screaming in agony and finally plunged out the window into the crowd below.

When she hit the ground, her flaming head separated from her body and rolled away in the night like a fiery little dandelion, chased by Cookies, who barked as the head bounced, nipped at it, and whimpered when it burnt his snout.

The villagers worked feverishly to extinguish the body as the prostitutes raced out of the brothel to help.

Volushka crept quietly out of the destruction of the room and down the stairs. He ran out the front door of the brothel and then ran around the back to make it appear like he came from the street. He moved along the outside of the circle, trying to get a better view of the scene.

Rutchka's body was charred and smoking, with most of her black bones and viscera exposed. Ashes and embers fluttered in the air and an awful stink issued out of her neck.

The crowd parted to let Doctor Klaschke in, and he knelt down to examine her. The villagers crowded at his shoulder, aghast. The acrid smoke burned his eyes.

"There's no doubt about it. She was poisoned."

The crowd gasped and many of the women started screaming.

Volushka looked up to Heaven in strained disbelief.

8 SPECTRES IN THE BEDCHAMBER

As the crowd thrilled in their suspicion and rising vengeance, Volushka quickly snuck away and ran to the *Uphegia* fields to hide. He crouched behind the giant stalks at the edge to keep an eye on the street, ready to run from a torchlight mob; nothing is more atmospheric and exciting to people than a night hunt and the mood was right for an especial orgy of violence.

He did not see Marcabrusa at the brothel and hoped the suspicion would fall on him. But the fact that he had to sleep with Witches, eat slugs and hide after midnight in the fields told Volushka that he would probably be the principal suspect. Marcabrusa would simply dazzle the villagers with some light remark and the fawning wind would fumble over itself to assist by blowing his forelock over his glittering eyes, and the next thing you know, Volushka would be running around the houses and through the streets. It was grossly unfair, even though this particular disgusting tragedy was Volushka's fault.

He saw a slug on a leaf and in his insulted pride, decided not to eat it.

The outcry and energy of the crowd lasted for almost an hour before people began to tire and disperse. He watched them disappear in little wayward groups, cursing, laughing, and wrestling with each other like drunken harpies. The night eventually became quiet, the streets empty. He relaxed in the peace, watching contentedly the lights of little candles flicker like stars from the different windows and then, with a yawn, one by one go out.

He was able to emerge from the *Uphegia* and stretch. It had been a hellish night and his head throbbed with the frustrating fact that he would have to somehow figure out how to use this charm before putting his full scheme in action. It was decidedly not the plan to have a village of screaming lunatics jumping out of windows on fire with burning heads rolling down the street.

Was he perhaps tricked by the Witch, embittered by her circumstances and malevolent by nature, giving him instead a charm to destroy him, and the whole village with him? Didn't he hold up his end of the bargain with another ecstatic, amorous and spiritually satisfying sexual performance? Why can't Witches be sensible or otherwise decent? Do they have to be hateful idiots all the time? Was that a Witch in that tree?!

He thought about abandoning the plan and just murdering Marcabrusa in his sleep. Surely, he could overcome him while Marcabrusa was unconscious.

On further thought, Volushka decided to be cautious. The way the Fates favored Marcabrusa, Volushka would probably fall through the floor or unfold his own intestines just as he was attacking his sleeping foe.

Apparently, he overestimated Rutchka's animal constitution and gave her too much. The Witch gave him a lot of powder, probably from gratitude, so he can conduct his plan village wide, not because he needed to administer generously. This was an infernal malefaction, imbued with a staggering power, probably from the Devil himself; he would need to exercise a little more prudence when using the powder next time.

Another test was clearly necessary.

Volushka walked around in the still night, alive in its peace and silence, owning the village. He scanned the quiet, dark houses until he came to the house of Mr. and Mrs. Wlawicka.

Those two scabrous imbeciles deserved to be afflicted with his charm, he thought, for all the grief they'd given Volushka over the years, especially that crone who was always threatening to call the villagers to thrash him for no other reason than for being a slob and existing. There's nothing Volushka would love to do more than shove her up his own ass, for all the sorrow it would cause her. And a sober observer would admit that Volushka would actually be doing a service for Mr. Wlawicka to have him buried alive, which would give him some much-needed peace from his sneer-bitching wife.

Volushka crept up to the house and worked at a locked door at the back with no success. He tried prying open a window but he bent his fingers backward, and he staggered around cursing with two throbbing, useless hands.

For some desperate reason, he thought he could fit through the transom window around front and carried a barrel of rainwater to the door to climb. Naturally, he fell off the barrel onto his face and the water spilled over him in a great, frigid wave. In his frustration, he resolved to simply throw the barrel through the door but when he tried to lift it over his head, he hurt his back and dropped it on his feet.

He finally managed by some supernatural inspiration, agency and effort to squeeze himself under a space in the foundation and find some loose floorboards in the kitchen that he could push up and out of the way. Soaked and dirty, he traipsed all the bugs, leaves and muck through the house as he made his way upstairs to the bedroom.

There were the awful Wlawickas, snoring and gaping like two ejaculating sharks.

He crept silently on his hands and knees to Mr. Wlawicka's side of the bed where, on the nightstand, was a small glass of cider. He stayed low to the ground, feeling on top of the nightstand for the glass, when Mr. Wlawicka stirred and briefly woke, before quickly going back to sleep, resuming his awful noises.

Volushka quickly laid face-down flat on the ground until he was sure Mr. Wlawicka was asleep again. After five minutes, he popped his head up to check on him when, to his absolute consternation and horror, Volushka saw Benzi looking at him from Mrs. Wlawicka's side of the bed.

Volushka went back to ground and let out a silent scream. He bit his fist in a boiling rage and then looked to Heaven for aid, for answers, for an explosive, fatal heart attack. He peeked up again across the bed and Benzi waved.

Volushka silently mouthed the words, *What the Hell are you doing here??*

Benzi mouthed back, *What are you doing here?*

O, for God's sakes! Get the Hell out of here!

You get the Hell out of here!

No, you get out of here!

You first!

Please!

What?

I said, Please go home!

I can't hear you.

I'm going to kill you!

I don't know what you're saying.

I'M. GOING. TO. KILL. YOU.

I DON'T KNOW.

Volushka pointed at Benzi and then frantically pointed to the door.

Benzi pointed back at Volushka and sternly did the same.

Volushka shook his fist at him.

Benzi returned the gesture.

Volushka threatened to strangle him.

Benzi threatened to shout.

Volushka begged him desperately not to do so.

Benzi took a deep breath in preparation to yell.

Volushka begged even more fervently, putting his hands together in prayer and shaking inconsolably.

Benzi leaned in to Mrs. Wlawicka and put his hand to his mouth as if to shout in her ear.

Volushka stared at him.

At that moment, Mr. Wlawicka's snoring woke him and he sat up in bed. Volushka went to the floor and closed his eyes. Mr. Wlawicka looked confusedly around the room, took a small sip of the cider, looked at his wife with nausea and then laid back down to sleep.

Volushka cautiously raised from the floor and eyed Mr. Wlawicka, ready to dive at a moment. When he was sure he was asleep, he looked across the bed for Benzi but, to his amazed delight, he was gone. He made little clicks and whistles to try and catch Benzi's attention but there was no response. Benzi was apparently frightened by Mr. Wlawicka and ran away, Heaven, for once, inflicting on that idiot child some common sense. What the Hell that asshole was doing up in the middle of the night was beyond all understanding; Volushka suspected that he wasn't actually a boy but some possessed little night salamander that only crawled out of his fire to vex good and decent folk out of their wits. It would only be right to slap the shit out of him the next time he saw him.

Volushka reached into his pocket to grab the Witch's powder and crept along like a serpent toward the nightstand and the little glass of cider. He would sprinkle in a pinch as a test and tickle Mr. Wlawicka's chin to try to get him to wake and have a drink. If he didn't leap out of the window on fire or otherwise destroy the place, Volushka could sprinkle in a little more into Mrs. Wlawicka's horrible, yawning maw. If all went well, he could then go to the graveyard and listen to see if they would wake in their graves.

Then he could leave them there and begin his plan in earnest.

As Volushka raised his hand to the glass, he felt a tap on his behind.

He turned to see Benzi on his hands and knees with an innocent little grin.

Volushka grabbed him by his shirt and whispered forcefully, *You little runt, how the Hell did you get in here? You need to go home right now, you're going to get us both in trouble!*

What are you doing here?

None of your business! It's late in the poisonous night, why the Hell aren't you in bed?!

One of the ladies went on fire and I couldn't sleep.

You saw it?

Yes, my sisters didn't want to leave me alone in the house because of goblins and so they brought me. I was right up front! She was gross and Cookies chased her head!

That's a fine thing bringing an already fractured lunatic to see an incinerated prostitute, no wonder you're such a hellish thing! Well, you've had enough stimulation for one night, now get out of here and go home!

Why don't you go home?

I'm going to right after I do something important, and I need total concentration, and especially tight reflexes, to pull this off, I can't have you getting me all coiled up!

Like with Rutchka.

What? No! Don't you start casting aspersions! That's how rumors get started and people get killed!

O for God's sakes...

Look, I'll buy you a sweet tomorrow if you'll just go home quietly.

Two sweets.

You — ok, two sweets!

With jelly.

With jelly!

And you have to carry me on your back all week and run fast.

I'm not some kind of pleasure animal! You get two sweets and that's it!

With jelly.

With jelly!

And you have to carry me on your back and run fast.

God dammit, ok! Now, go home!

I want to stay and watch.

O my God! You son of a bitch!

Mrs. Wlawicka started murmuring in her sleep and Volushka and Benzi huddled close like two quiet mice. They looked at each other with excited dread and then Benzi popped up to watch Mrs. Wlawicka until she went down into her rattling sleep.

Benzi gave Volushka the all-clear sign and Volushka turned back to the nightstand. He looked at the glass of cider anxiously, then to Mr. Wlawicka nervously, his hands sweating. After all of the arguing and near discoveries, he started to quail about the plan and thought it ultimately best to sneak out of the room to regroup, preferably on a night without Benzi.

He turned around to Benzi pointing at Mr. Wlawicka, nodding his head in encouragement.

Volushka turned again to the nightstand confused and Benzi jumped on his back to help. Volushka took a pinch of powder out of his pouch and reached for the cider glass. Just as he was about to sprinkle it in, Mr. Wlawicka roused from sleep to get out of bed and kicked Volushka in the head when he tried to step on the floor.

Mr. Wlawicka started screaming in anger, waking the fiery Mrs. Wlawicka, who leapt out of bed like a hallucinating orangutan. Volushka, with Benzi on his back, tried to silence the two with desperate pleas for a moment to explain, recognizing how, in the quiet of the night, the shouting and commotion seemed to carry far and wide across the village. The Wlawickas, however, were not interested in this two-headed intruder's excuses or explanations and somehow started yelling even louder. Mr. Wlawicka began punching the big head while Mrs. Wlawicka was biting him and now Volushka was adding to the demented chorus, crying out in agony as Benzi giggled uncontrollably. When Mrs. Wlawicka realized that this wasn't some deformed monster from the marshes and saw Benzi waving at her, she stopped biting Volushka and pulled Benzi off his back, cuddling him close and screaming for help out the window. Mr. Wlawicka and Volushka wrestled and started crashing around the room, his wife's hysterical screaming rousing the villagers from their beds. About ten families ran to the Wlawickas' house, kicked down the door and ran upstairs just as Mr. Wlawicka and Volushka were strangling themselves with the bedsheets. The men parted the two combatants and held Volushka under guard while the women huddled around Mrs. Wlawicka and Benzi, trying to console them.

"What the Hell is happening tonight?!" the Cooper said in exhausted exasperation. "People being poisoned in the middle of the night, heads rolling around the streets on fire, bedroom brawling with a spastic Mastodon, how the Hell does anyone get any sleep around here?"

"There's a miasma and it's corrupting everything! The graves are unlocking and all manner of unnatural events are happening! We're doomed!" cried Mrs. Saskoveska, and the women all joined her in their terror.

"I want to know what this disgusting imbecile is doing in my house!" shouted Mr. Wlawicka.

"And with this sweet little boy!" added his wife and all the women sighed over him, stroked his hair, and moved in close to protect him.

"What happened, Benzi? How did you get here?" asked Florya, the Miller's wife.

"Did that dirty slob drag you here?" asked Glasha, glowering at Volushka.

"Was it witchcraft?" asked Mrs. Saskoveska in her attention-craving hysterics.

"I don't know, I got confused," said Benzi in a sad little voice.

All the women fawned over him.

"O! He got confused! The poor thing!"

"Of course, he got confused! It's dark and scary outside!"

"O my goodness!"

"What an angel, the poor dear!"

"Somebody go downstairs and get him a cookie, next to my pestles," said Mrs. Wlawicka, swaying Benzi in her arms. "Would you like a cookie, darling?"

"Yes, because I got confused."

"Hurry, Glasha!"

Glasha ran downstairs and quickly returned with a yummy thing as big as his head. Benzi was passed into Suba's arms, and he ate it in little bites with his little mouth as the women swooned over him.

"That explains how he got here, but now why is this filthy asshole here?!" shouted Mr. Wlawicka.

"Don't you frighten Benzi! And do not use that language!" countered Mrs. Wlawicka and she squared her shoulders to pounce and smash him in the head.

"I'm sorry, Benzi, I'm just upset because it's late and a lot of awful things have happened, including wrestling around the room with this asshole!"

"Volka!!" shouted Mrs. Wlawicka and she slapped him so that his head slumped over his shoulder.

Volushka, still restrained by the men and tangled in the bedsheet, wriggled around in exasperation while trying to defuse the whole situation.

"We all need to be calm, especially as we're plagued by so many strange events and awful omens, and we have to stand together as a village if we're going to ward off these evil things. Believe me, I'm frightened, too. Can you let me go?! And this damn thing…. I'm not trying to honeyfuggle anyone, and I'm not here with malintent, the only reason all of the furniture is broken is because this guy just attacked me and didn't give me any chance to explain! I saw from afar the awful thing that happened to poor Rutchka and I have been sleepless because of it. While watching out for all manner of spectres and devils, I happened to see Benzi wandering around confused in the dead of night, and I followed him into the Wlawickas' house so I could bring him home safely when, all of a sudden, Wlawicka erupted in a lunatic fury and attacked me. I'm not saying I blame you, Volka, I'm sure it was a surprise to see me here and a sensible man would defend his hearth but if you could have just given me a moment to explain, all of this could have been avoided and these good people would be snuggled down at home as we speak. If you still thought I was a threat then you could have punched me in the face or worse, had Mrs. Wlawicka slap my head upside-down."

"Don't think I still won't, you're a slithering one and should be killed! Is that what happened, Benzi, did you get confused and wander up here? You won't get in trouble, sweetie, we just want to know if you're ok and make sure we get you home where it's safe and warm," and Mrs. Wlawicka's eyes glistered with the peace of the lily as she spoke to him.

"That's exactly what happened, and I came over to help him!" Volushka shouted in exasperation.

The women all started screaming at Volushka and the men started pushing him around in a circle.

"You shut up! Nobody needs to hear anything from you!" Mrs. Wlawicka turned back to Benzi. "Is that what happened, you got lost, Darling, and Volushka showed up to help?"

"I don't know because I got all confused. I think so…"

"You poor thing, that's ok, baby."

"…But it doesn't seem likely."

The women as one body, and all at once, glared at Volushka and then set their fierce gaze onto their husbands who, after an instant of panic, slowly realized that they should already be beating up Volushka and now knew in their loins the consequences of not starting straightaway. They turned on Volushka with seething anger for nearly getting them killed.

"What? No! Wait a minute! He obviously doesn't know what he's saying, clearly he's still confused! Come on, there's no way you can't see that! Now listen! Wait! Dammit, he does this shit all the time! O, COME ON!"

The women watched with a lusty, spiritually satisfied vengeance as the men kicked the living shit out of him.

Benzi looked on from Suba's arms, eating his cookie.

9 OSCULATIONS OF THE LITTLE AND THE DOOMED

"O, no you don't, you're no longer allowed to sit here!"

"Yes, I can! It's my log, too!"

"No, it's not! Go anyplace else, I'm not speaking to you!"

"Why not?"

"WHY NOT? O my God! You know exactly why not!"

"Is it because you shit your pants?"

"You get out of here!"

"Do you want some slugs?"

"No, stop talking to me!"

"Is it because you look stupid all over the place?"

"I'm warning you, you're this close to being strangled!"

"Well, why are you so cruddy?"

"O for God sakes!"

"What?"

"You ruined the whole thing!"

"I did not! Ruined what?"

"Don't you pretend you don't remember what happened just last night!"

"I'm not pretending! There was a lot that happened to me to remember!"

"To you?? What happened to you other than being cuddled and having a cookie?"

"See how hard it is to remember everything?"

"Please just go home!"

"Why?"

"You stupid bastard, we had it! We could have just floated out of there, free as a breeze, all you had to do was just say you were confused and I helped you and it all would have been fine! But as long as you have a cookie, you're just thrilled watching everyone else go to Hell!"

"I did say I was confused!"

"I'm not talking to you, you idiot!"

"I don't understand why you're cross all the time, I'm not the one who deformed you!"

"I wouldn't *be* deformed if you would stop getting me beat up all the time!"

"Yes, you would!"

"NO, I WOULDN'T! You just enjoy my misery, like some sort of little demon frog!"

"I like frogs."

"I don't care if you like frogs! I'm not talking to you ever again!"

"Frogs are known to make ribbit sounds."

"You just shut up!"

"You're mad because I had a cookie?"

"I'm mad because you didn't choke to death on it!"

"I was going to give you a bite but you were in some sort of reverse neck crunch!"

"And why do you think *that was*?"

"Because you're always in a reverse neck crunch?"

"No, because of you!"

"That doesn't seem likely…"

"You son of a bitch. You big dumb son of a bitch! What kind of soulless animal are you?"

"If I were an animal, I would be a Basilisk because he could pretty much gnash everybody's face off. Or a bunny."

"You're neither, you're a pain-in-the-ass runt!"

"I wish I knew what you were talking about half the time, but it's all just stupid shouting. Are you grouchy because your face is falling off?"

"I'm not going in these circles with you just so you can have a grand old time annoying me!"

"Why didn't you just fight back and beat everybody up?"

"I can't just beat up fifty people all the time!"

"There was only like ten guys there!"

"Ten guys is plenty! And I was tangled in a bedsheet!"

"Maybe you would do better if you punched people with your fists and not your face."

"I wasn't punching them with my face!"

"Not only were you punching them with your face, you were punching them in their fists. You should hit them in the head, that seems to work on you."

"I'm going to hit you in the head!"

"Gross."

"Why is that gross?"

"I don't want to get your face all over me!"

"I WOULDN'T HIT YOU WITH MY FACE!"

"It's like all mushy!"

"You moron! You just eat away at my guts all day!"

"Do you just want to cry a little bit so you can feel better?"

"No, I don't!"

"I won't look and if I start laughing it's because I'm thinking of something else funny."

"No, you know what, I'm leaving. You can laugh yourself all the way to the Devil for all I care! I'm through with you!"

Volushka strained with all his bruises to get up from the log and, after taking a couple of wobbly steps, slumped back down to rest. He refused to look at Benzi who was staring at him with little giggly eyes.

It was at that moment that Vulga and Groska Bulgy-Ogrova, little blonde eight-year-old twins, showed up in pretty, white lace dresses and with shy, little laughter.

Vulga whispered into Groska's ear and then Groska said, "Hi, Benzi!" in a sweet and playful voice.

"Ugh, Hi, Groska, what do you want?"

"Vulga likes you!"

"Ok, well, I'm pretty busy."

"Doing what?"

"All sorts of muscular stuff, I can't explain it all to a bunch of silly girls."

"You look like you're just sitting there with a gorilla."

"Hey!"

"I'll handle this…. That's right and he's just about to cry and make another mess in his pants so you better get out of here so he can feel better."

"Ok, but can Vulga have another kiss first?"

"What?! No! What do you mean?"

Volushka loomed over Benzi with fresh new reserves of spirit and malicious joy, all the pain of his body instantly vanishing like a tickled purple smoke.

"OOOOOOOOOOO!!!"

"What?! No!"

"OOOOOOOOOOOOOOOOOOOOOOOOOO!!!!"

"O gross, I did not!"

Volushka put his hands to his heart and made smoochy noises, fluttering as best as he could the one eye that wasn't entirely swollen shut.

"O for God sakes!"

"OOOOOOOOOOOOOOOOOOOOOOOOOOO!!!"
More smoochy noises.
"NO! I DID NOT! NO!"
"O thank you, God! Finally! For once!! OOOOOOO!!"
"NO WAY! O MY GOD!!"
"OOOOOOOOOOOO, Love me, love me, love me!"
Benzi now stood up on the log as the girls laughed and got up right in Volushka's face.

"You know what happened was? I was running around! (*And then looking at the girls*) And I know I'm not supposed to be running around. (*Back to Volushka*) When I turned and all of a sudden, she crashed into me! And our lips......... grazed. She grazed me! I didn't kiss nobody, I was grazed! And then *that* one went running around telling tales!"

"OOOOOOOOOOOOOOOOOOOOOOOOOO!!!"

"O my God! NO! NO!! And you both have to get out of here, go away! I'm a boy and not playing with girls! Just go someplace else!"

"Ok, Benzi. I love you!" Vulga said and the girls ran away giggling.

"Ok, I'll see you later," Benzi said.

"OOOOOOOOOOOOOOOOOOOOOOOOOO!!!!"

"O, Come on!"

"O Benzi, I love you! I want to kiss you again and again! O smoochy kisses, let's get married and be in love forever!"

"O gross! No way! I don't even like her, she's ugly!"

"OOOOOOOOOOOOOOOOOOOOOOOOOO!!!"

"I like the other one!"

"OO — what?!"

"She's gross!"

"What do you mean you like the other one? They're exactly the same!"

"What?"

"Are you being thick on purpose?! They're twins, what the Hell are you talking about she's ugly, there's no way to tell them… apart…." And with that thought, Volushka drifted again into another one of his faraway reveries, into a world of devious inspirations and cunning schemes, where he saw with malicious purpose a plan to turn the tables and restore the order to the good, in one last grandiose wager. This new ploy would accomplish the whole wonderful plan in one, spectacular showdown, without the horrible uncertainties of trying to poison twelve different imbeciles, in favor of a direct contest between Volushka and that loathsome Marcabrusa which would demonstrate verily and finally who was the better and rightful possessor of place. And once the village could see easily and indisputably who was the born Grave Listener and who was the fraud, it would surely be a simple tip of logic to see that it was Marcabrusa, the conniving stranger, who was the person to be driven out or hanged for this whole terrible misfortune.

Volushka could feel his liver tickle with joy, and he reveled again and again in the little scene of his triumph, carried aloft on the shoulders of a grateful village, down the hill and through the cemetery gates.

Benzi waited yet again for Volushka to return from his ogrish little daydream, shaking his head at his twisting expressions as they cycled through evil plotting and dreamy, victorious celebrations. When this spell seemed to be in another eternal loop, he slapped him in the head until Volushka recovered his present senses.

Volushka looked at him with bewildered vexation.

Benzi simply nodded, very slowly, with a much malicious grin.

10 SCHEMES OF AN ABSOLUTE HORROR

Volushka, Benzi and Bunny skulked all over the village, around, between and behind the brothel, the Milliner's, the Cooper's, Mrs. Jarmulka's pie shop, the Tanner's and back to the brothel, as they worked their inspired way to the Undertaker's. When they were nearly discovered, peeping out of an alley, they moved secretly like a mist around the periphery of the village, stealing apples from Bokuva's orchard and a milk pail at Ludokowa's farm, finally hiding in one of the stables of Maroska Kepkovic to have a quick nibble and go over the plan.

"You're getting apples and milk all over yourself!" Benzi said with disgusted delight.

"You're about to get milk and shut up all over *yourself!*"

"You eat like you have two assholes!"

"How would you like a punch in the face? You know what, I don't even care, I've got the larger universe on my mind right now! I have to focus on the plan designs!"

"And what are the plan designs?"

"Can you keep a secret?"

"No."

"For God's sakes, then I'm not telling you!"

"That's because you don't have the plan designs."

"I have the plan designs!"

"No, you don't."

"Yes, I do!"

"No, you don't."

"The plan is one of the most brilliant things you would have ever heard!"

"The plan is full of holes!"

"You don't even know what the plan is!"

"Neither do you!"

"I do so! Mostly! And it involves your girlfriends!"

"I know, I had to sit through another one of your evil spells after they left."

"I wasn't having a spell!"

"You had a fart face for about twenty minutes!"

"I don't have fart faces!"

"It's like your ass is on your neck!"

"How was it possible for you to cram so much shittiness into that little body in five years?!"

"I don't know, how was it possible for you to cram six apples into your mouth in three minutes?"

"I'm going to bust your face!"

"I'm going to bust your whole entire head!"

"Can't you just shut up and let me have an apple and five minutes of peace?"

"How is that going to help?"

"It'll help me clear my mind and concentrate on the plan designs for starters!"

"Ok, well, go ahead!"

"Then be quiet!"

"I am being quiet! So, what are the plan designs?"

"Ok, look — Marcabrusa has used some kind of witchcraft to confuse the villagers and raise a plague that is causing people to die, then he's waking them and garnering the glories in my place, which has quite put a death sentence on me…"

"Yeah, he's pretty smart."

"No, he isn't! Anyway, I'm not going to best him with my beauty or charm…"

"Holy shit, no."

"Stop interrupting me! And we're pretty evenly matched when it comes to strength and don't even say anything! So, I'll have to outwit him and beat him at the one thing I'm best at, which is Grave Listening, exposing him for the mountebank he is. Therefore, I intend to challenge him to a Listening duel, using two girls of the same make and constitution to rule out any kind of circumstance or advantage in the result; and the one who saves the girl will be clearly known to be the one anointed by God as the rightful man and the other a fraud, a pestilence, a thing of sorcery to be destroyed!"

"And you're going to give them the plague?"

"Well, not this plague, in its present variety…"

"And how are you going to win? Marcabrusa has been waking everybody!"

"When I defeated the Witch of Gore Mal Gore, I took this magical powder. It suspends the life of anyone who takes it, and makes them the very resemblance of death, to go so far as to even fool Galen himself. I will give this powder to the one girl, and the fatal black Night Gruesome to the other and the one will wake and the other won't. That's when Marcabrusa will be dragged to the Gallows, hanged, then cut into pieces and scattered!"

"Well, if they'll both look the same…"

"They'll both look the same!"

"Well, if they'll both look the same, how will you know which one's yours?"

"That's why we have to go to the Undertaker, to bring his hand into the plan."

"He's not going to help you, he hates your guts!"

"He'll help me! He's a greasy old snake, he'll do anything for a few dolmarks! He's burying them anyway, it's nothing more to do for him to get some extra money! Besides, he can get paid for the one girl twice."

"I think he's just going to punch you in your balls."

"He's not going to punch me in my balls! All he has to do is fix a white flower to my coffin and a red flower to Marcabrusa's and he'll walk away with an extra ten dolmarks!"

"Twenty."

"Ten! Who the Hell are you, his solicitor?!"

"Does that magic powder even work?"

"Of course, it does! It's Witchery!"

"Well, how do you know?"

"I just know!"

"Ok, but Rutchka's head went rolling down the street."

"What does that have to do with anything? Rutchka's an idiot!"

"They're going to be pretty hard to wake when they don't have any heads on them."

"They're going to have heads on them!"

"I'm pretty sure at least one of them is not going to have a head."

"They're going to have heads!"

"Prove it!"

"What do you mean, prove it?"

"Try it out!"

"On whom?"

"On that horse!"

"That's ridiculous! It's not the same thing!"

"I thought it was Witchery!"

"It is!"

"Then why won't it work?"

"It'll work but people and horses are two different things, I don't exactly know how this stuff is rated for horses, it's completely different ratios!"

"Are you afraid his head is going to explode and fly across the room?"

"You'd love that, wouldn't you! …All right, stand back, you rotten tempter! You're just so damn smart, about everything, aren't you? …All I wanted to do was eat some apples, now I'm poisoning a horse! I hope *your* head pops off!"

Volushka walked around the stable looking nervously at the different horses until he came to a stall where a giant, black horse looked back at him with hissing revulsion. Insulted, Volushka sprinkled some powder on an apple and gave it to the horse, who ate it greedily. The two stared at each other silently for almost ten minutes, the horse sneering at Volushka while he waited impatiently for the horse's head to fall off.

Nothing happened.

"Isn't he supposed to be dead?"

"No, he's supposed to resemble death!"

"Well, he's not resembling it."

"I can see that! His head's still on, though."

"Maybe you have to give him more."

"I can't just give him all my poison, I've got to save some for the children!"

"Well, it doesn't seem like it works."

"It works! He's just a dumb horse!"

"He's too dumb to be poisoned?"

"He's just dumb, that's all! His head didn't explode, that's enough!"

"But if the girl doesn't resemble, how will you beat Marcabrusa?"

"Dammit, give me another apple!"

Volushka sprinkled even more powder on it and fed the horse the second apple. The horse swallowed it in three bites, shook its head with a little frisson of joy and then stared at Volushka with bottomless contempt.

"He likes apples!" Benzi chortled.

"What the Hell is wrong with this supernatural horse? Is he Jesus Christ?"

"He doesn't look like he *feels* like dying."

"Maybe if I punched him in his disgusted face!"

"Are you sure you beat up a Witch? Maybe it was just some ugly guy?"

"It *was* a Witch! Don't make me kick you in the mouth!"

"What if you strangled him a little first and *then* gave him an apple?"

"How do you strangle someone a little? Are you stupid?"

"Hug him like you love him with your arms and legs really hard but just for like five seconds."

"And my legs? That's ridiculous, you want me to straddle his face? I'm not going to try and strangle a horse with my balls in his mouth! Why am I listening to you?!"

Suddenly, the horse reared up and, pissing and screaming, turned and kicked the stall front off its hinges, smashing it into Volushka and knocking him to the ground as he covered up Benzi to shield him. The horse then galloped out of the stable shaking its head violently.

"Where the Hell is he going?!" Volushka shouted, throwing the stall front off of them.

"He went crazy!"

"He was an asshole!"

"I'm not sure this stuff works."

"It works! It just means you can't oversprinkle it, I'll give them just a couple of grains. We'd better get out of here, Maroska and his men will be coming."

Volushka, Benzi and Bunny snuck out of the back of the stable and ran into the surrounding forest, the sound of the farm folk raising alarms behind them. As they quickly made their way toward the Undertaker, Benzi tugged on the back of Volushka's pants.

"Excuse me?"

"Don't slow me down, what do you want now? And it better not be something that aggravates me! Just keep running or go home!"

"I'm not aggravating! But I don't know about the plan designs, how are you going to poison the girls?"

"That part is tricky, I obviously can't just walk into their house and slap some powder into their heads. I don't have a lot of access to them. I'm sure if I had the diabolic persuasions of Marcabrusa, I could just waltz through the door and poison them right in front of their family, but I'm not in league with his devils!"

"Why'd you pick the stupid ones?"

"I'm not in league with any ones!"

"Except a Witch."

"That was a one-time transaction! In a special case, against a satanic adversary, with larger consequences in the balance! You couldn't possibly understand the moral and human intricacies involved here, the overall concitations of human nature, so don't even start on me!"

"I'm pretty sure I've seen them."

"You don't know the first thing! You're always talking nonsense and twisting everything around, especially my balls! There are a whole host of fires and fustigans in human nature that hurl life headlong into the dust and we are in a fatal battle with them, and because of that, you have to understand the poetry of the thing!"

"And what's the poetry of the thing?"

"Don't you worry about it!"

"So, you don't know the poetry of the thing."

"I do so!"

"No, you don't."

"I do so! Stop wrenching my balls!"

"No, you don't."

"For God's sakes! You can just go on and on forever, picking at me without rest! You're going to be a great torturer in Hell!"

"That's because you don't know the poetry of the thing."

Volushka stopped and turned, staring for a moment at Benzi and Bunny with a frigid intensity. They looked back at him placidly, with their invisible smile of eternal peace.

"The poetry is a tale whose tragic hero is human nature. And that's the end of it."

"Ok," Benzi said, shrugging his shoulders.

Volushka turned again and stormed away. Benzi and Bunny followed.

"Well, without Marcabrusa's diabolic persuasions, you're still in trouble, how are you going to get at the girls?"

"I'll think of something."

"You should probably have the plan designs before you speak to the Undertaker."

"I suppose I will, I just need time to think."

"Is there any way you can get Marcabrusa's diabolic persuasions?"

"The only diabolic thing I know is you."

"And the only diabolic thing *I* know is *you*!"

"Well, then we're stuck with each other. But as diabolic persuasions go, you're without a doubt the worst."

"I'm better than Marcabrusa's!"

"Well, that's no real victory! Although, come to think of it, perhaps that is…"

"See!"

"I don't have any access to the girls, but you do. Didn't you get all sloppy lips with one of them and fall madly in love together?"

"NO! I did not! I pretty much explained that already, but you're just a stupid jerk all day!"

"Which one was it?"

"Vulga."

"What a pretty name."

"No, it isn't, it's gross! Just like her!"

"Marcabrusa may have the Devil, but I have you. You can be the Love Bait."

"I'm not Love Bait!"

"That's your new nickname."

"No, it isn't!"

"Yes, it is."

"No, it isn't!!"

"Yes, it is."

"NO, IT'S NOT!!"

"Yes, it is."

"YOU SHUT UP!!"

"Listen, Love Bait, you owe me, for all the times you've gotten me in trouble and beaten half to death. I've had to put up with you for all too long, you've been no end of aggravation, and for all your wickedness, Mr. Love Bait, now is the time to pay that debt!"

"I hate you, I won't help at all!"

"O, well! Love Bait can call me fat and stupid all day but faced with the prospect of having the whole village know you were kissing a girl, now the whole thing is unfair! Poor, Mr. Love Bait!"

"STOP CALLING ME THAT!!" And Benzi folded his arms and started to cry.

Volushka stood in confused silence as Benzi sobbed dearly. He finally knelt before him and put his hand on his shoulder as Benzi hid his face behind Bunny.

"I'm sorry. I didn't mean it. I won't do it again. I just said it like we were playing because you're my friend."

Volushka, Benzi and Bunny then hugged each other for a long time so they could let Benzi finish his crying.

11 COFFERS AND COFFINS

The only reason the Undertaker didn't slam the door in Volushka's face was because Benzi was with him, carried on his back.

He looked at the boy and shook his head in sad, disgusted disbelief.

"Still hanging around with this boy. I'm going to quite enjoy your execution, you actually make me sick. And if I haven't made it impossibly clear, I don't want to be seen associating with you so get the Hell out of here before I drag you to the Gallows myself. The next time I want to see you is when I'm measuring you for a box."

"There's no reason to be so morose all the time!"

"I'm an Undertaker, it's my job to be morose."

"Well, I'm not exactly fond of you, but I can still be cordial."

"Now that we've established our feelings for each other, you can go kill yourself somewhere else."

"Listen, I just need five minutes of your time."

"There's nothing I can do for you."

"There's something very simple you can do for me…"

"I won't do it anyway. And I won't do it just to spite you."

"Would you not do it to spite your coffer?"

The Undertaker just stared coldly.

"Look, I have a proposition to make you a little extra on a small endeavor that will require you to do absolutely nothing more than you're already doing. Nothing else."

"You want to pay me extra to do nothing?"

"Just to fix a flower to a coffin. That's it."

"So, all the kicks in the head have now made you sentimental?"

"Do you want some money or don't you?"

The Undertaker reluctantly stood aside to let them in.

"Put the boy down and tell me who it is that has earned such an affectionate gesture. I assume being acquainted with you killed them."

"They're not quite dead yet."

"They."

"You can't have failed to notice the effects that Marcabrusa and his plague have brought to the village, how many people have died since he came here."

"I'm an Undertaker, I like when people die."

"Well, he's also somehow waking them and now that Marcabrusa's around to save them, I've heard fools at the brothel say that they're not going to pay for your sacred pomp and craft for loved ones who are only down for a few days, they'll just bury them in an old blanket themselves. Something wicked is clearly happening and it's in your interests, I would think, that you would want it to end."

"And in yours that this handsome, charming and utterly competent rival is dead."

"Naturally, so why not work together to restore both of our fortunes?"

"Because I can't stand you and wish you were dead. Marcabrusa's success, and his good standing in the village, will all but assure that you're killed. I told him that if he promised not to listen by your grave, I would pay him, but he reminded me that no one would ask him to do so."

"And then you'll have this utterly competent Adonis possibly spoiling your business for years, how many times were *you* kicked in the head?"

"I will deal with Marcabrusa when the time is right."

"You will, really? Because you're so suave and smart and martial? If you don't wake up now, you'll be poor and in the street! And I'm sure, in your vanity and your disesteem of me, that you feel you would need no effort at all to dispatch me whenever you wanted, why not take on the stronger man first with an ally?"

"No."

"Why not??"

"Because I can see you desperately want me to help you and I want you to suffer."

"You stupid bastard!"

"You think I would trust you? You're an idiot, you couldn't possibly outwit this man or have any ability or grace to overcome him. Why would I tie your millstone around my neck?"

"I have a plan aided by the dark arts, more powerful and cunning than any saint of a man can withstand!"

"I find that hard to believe."

"Well, then look at this — this is a magical powder I procured from the Witch of Gore Mal Gore that can temporarily suspend a person's life and make them resemble death itself! The pale flesh, the black eyes, the suspension of breath, an imperceptible heartbeat! A magic from the very depths of Hell!"

"You're going to overcome Marcabrusa with some flour mixed with shoe black?"

"It's not flour!"

"You got so drunk, you broke into Mrs. Jarmulka's pie shop and stole some flour?"

"No! It was the real Witch! I nearly lost my life in combat with all the powers of the damned!"

"I'd have to be as stupid as you to believe that and only half as drunk."

"Well, have some if you think it's flour!"

"I wouldn't take anything from you."

"Well, if you're so sure! You can prove that I'm a liar!"

"I already know you're a liar."

"Then have some of this flour!"

"Don't be ridiculous."

"You're right to be afraid! This has powers beyond all mercy or help!"

"And it poisoned a horse!" Benzi offered, helpfully.

"Well, it's not for horses…"

"You used the magical powers of Hell on a horse?"

"It was a whole complicated affair that's beyond the point, but I hasten to note that the horse succumbed to its powers, and it was devastating!"

"And how do you expect to get Marcabrusa to take this magical flour from Hell without him shoving it up your ass?"

"It's not for him."

"Who's it for?"

"O, sure, I could easily kill Marcabrusa and end this plague right now but it's not going to vindicate me! He's been sowing discord and lies for the last month, impugning my abilities as a Grave Listener with his frauds, and otherwise destroyed my livelihood! He's stolen my birthright and poisoned the public trust, so that I'm a hunted animal, hiding in the forests and the mires like a monster!"

"The only thing he's done is to be handsome, sparkling and helpful."

"That's right, it's wickedness of the lowest orders! The only way to restore myself is to expose his frauds in a final professional contest of righteous judgment, before the village and the face of God, pitting my genuine Grave Listening license against his demonic dissembling!"

"And you think you'll best him? You truly are the stupidest person in the world."

"Of course not, not with his demonic charms behind him! Even as I'm the born Grave Listener, ordained by God, and provided for by right of lineage and custom, I wouldn't be able to overcome the advantages provided by his wicked helpers! So, it is only fair and fitting that I level the field so we can properly assess the actual merits of two equal men!"

"You really believe your own sophistry, don't you?"

"It's called Logica Nescia, it's a new discipline, I couldn't expect you to understand it!"

"And prayer is not an option to counter the works of the Devil?"

"Don't be stupid! That would take forever! And where the Hell is our new priest, anyway? It's the Church's fault that we're so vulnerable here!"

"In the interests of getting you out of my parlor, what exactly are you going to do?"

"What is required here is some way to objectively judge the actual skills and merits of the two opponents, stripping away all the variability that may confuse the proposition, favor one rival over the other or otherwise account for a random outcome; controlling for differences in age and morphology, relative health before death, manner of death, astrological influences, state of moral corruption, and the constitution of humors will help us focus solely on the properties specific to Grave Listening, which will prevent Marcabrusa from arguing his way out of defeat by unfair advantages! To that end, the best subjects would be the Bulgy-Ogrova twins, alike in every way, and ideal controls for such a contest. Because they're twins, we also know they are an inauspicious birth and most likely the reason why everything is in such busted kilter, so the death of one or both of them will, by itself, save us from absolute destruction."

"Wouldn't it just be easier to kill yourself?"

"Of course, it would be easier, but it would be completely unjust!"

"It would be the only thing that's just about this whole situation."

"What would you know about what's just or fair? Stop pretending you're some righteous saint walking above us in the clouds!"

"And the Bulgy-Ogrova twins have agreed to this contest?"

"Well, no, not in the consensual sense but as twins whose perverted birth has spoiled our crops and raised storms, their sacrifice for this village is one I am sure that they would spiritually approve for the expiation of their sins. Besides, only one of them will tender the last true measure of devotion, the other one will eventually be as right as rain!"

"If she recovers from the trauma of being buried alive."

"Exactly!"

"How comforting."

"The one girl will get the Witch's powder and the other will get the Night Gruesome. I'll give the Night Gruesome to the annoying one and that will make everyone feel better. All you need to do is fix a white flower to the ensorcelled coffin and a red flower to the Night Gruesome coffin. I'll handle the rest and give you ten dolmarks for nothing!"

"So, you're going to prove you're the superior Grave Listener, and Marcabrusa's a fraud, by perpetuating a fraud?"

"Just this one time!"

"And murder a child."

"These are extraordinary circumstances, I already explained that! After Marcabrusa, the villain working for the ruin of the *entire* village, is eliminated, I'll prove it in spades by my regular professional feats! For God's sakes, they're unnatural twins!"

"You are pathetic and perverse. Even if you convince these people that Marcabrusa is the cause of the plague and they kill him, nobody is going to vindicate you. I wish you the best of luck, I'll enjoy watching you get kicked in the face all over the street."

"What if I also promised you a cut of my earnings for each corpse I listen for going forward? Let's say, five percent goes back in your pocket as a small retainer."

"Eighty percent."

"What?!! Are you crazy?!"

"If you want me to remain quiet about you murdering one child and burying the other alive, you are going to pay for it."

"That's outrageous, you're robbing me blind! I can't live on what they pay me as it is!"

"I don't personally care."

"I'll give you fifteen percent! There's lots of people dying, these are evil times, fifteen percent will fatten you up plenty!"

"Eighty percent."

"O, come on! That's just stupid!"

"What's stupid is this idiotic plan, which makes no

sense and will fail spectacularly. I'm hoping in the end, of course, that you're entirely flayed alive."

"Forty percent and that's the final deal, you're not going to get better terms than that!"

"No. Get out of here and expect a ravenous mob to cut you to pieces after I disclose the vicious stupidity of your schemes. I'm not even going to bury you, I'll leave you to the dogs and your soul can wander restlessly around the cess pit where it belongs."

"Ok, eighty percent! You son of a bitch!"

"You bring the girls and the flowers. And get out."

"I guess it's not perverse at its price! You've got some balls sermonizing to me!"

"I'll take your point, perhaps the price of the perverse is dearer than that. Shall we say ninety percent?"

"No! I'm going! That's it! I'll be back with all the flowers!"

Volushka stormed out with Benzi doing his best to keep up. Out in the street, Volushka was purple with fury.

"I have half a mind to go back in there and slap his damned eyeballs to the other side of his head! Of all the ugly nerve! Who the Hell does he think he is?!"

"He's going to get a lot of money…"

"He's not getting a damned thing! I'll stab myself in the face before I pay him anything!"

"If you don't pay him, he's going to tell!"

"He's not going to be able to say anything. After he dresses my coffins, I'm going to handle him. You better go on home now, your sisters are sure to be worried. Stay away for the next day or so, I don't want you to get mixed up in it."

"Ok. Good-bye." And Benzi ran home.

"Good night, little Night Goblin."

12 TEMPTATION WITH BUTTERFLIES

It was washing day. The crisp morning sun brought forth all the autumn butterflies to the village well, circling around the bucket for their turn to alight and drink some water.

The early morning light was also sure to summon the women and young girls to collect their water for breakfast, for animals, for scrubbing their floors. The well was the place to wake, to work, to gossip.

Volushka usually knew better than to invade their space, as most men learned quite early the drenching consequences of interfering in the morning gathering, but with a new scheme in mind, today was a special day. He sat on the edge of the well dreamily, enjoying the butterflies, scattering them in a pretty cloud whenever he pulled the bucket for a drink.

Mrs. Wlawicka startled him out of a revery when she snatched the bucket out of his hand.

"Why the Hell are you here fouling the well?!"

He grabbed the bucket back out of her hands. "I'm just getting a drink! What the Hell are *you* doing here? I thought water rejected Witches?"

"Listen, you jack-ass, you're not allowed here! You

better leave right now or else I'm going to beat you senseless!"

"Just try it, you crone, and I'll kick you right in your balls!"

"How dare you! Get your filthy hands off this bucket!" She yanked the bucket out of his hands again and smashed him in the face with it.

"OW! You stupid hag!"

Volushka put her in a rear naked choke, then ripped the bucket out of her hands and tried stuffing her head in it. Mrs. Wlawicka, screaming at the top of her lungs, kicked Volushka repeatedly up and down his legs and punched at him wildly, finally grabbing his genitals until he let go. She hit him again and again with the bucket, chasing him as far as the rope would let. He ran and hid in an alley between the Cooper's and the Butcher's, with a headache nine miles nine.

He spied on the well from the alley, completely concussed, until the horrible Mrs. Wlawicka loped her beastly way back to her sulfurous lair.

The beautiful, sunny autumn morning was quiet again. Volushka limped his way back to the well to lave his wounds and get a fortifying drink.

The butterflies were now annoying, and he seethed in their lovely, delicate, little clouds.

He grumbled in his throbbing head, cursing life, nature, fate, the human design. He waited impatiently for the next woman to come and give him a cross look so he could throw a flying scissor kick right into her moldy face.

Perhaps the sunny morning, the sweet autumn air, made for lazy houses, or maybe the four-hundred-pound roaring of Mrs. Wlawicka frightened the women away, but the well was especially shy of visitors today. Volushka began to tire, and started to drift into a nap, dissolving into the introit of a dream that began with a topless Mrs. Wlawicka punching him in the face until he was rescued by a charming and worthy voice.

"Good morning. Well, I haven't seen you for quite a while, but my Lord! I'm sorry to see that you're looking so rough. Did you just crawl out of the well? Or do you need help getting back in?"

Marcabrusa put his hand on Volushka's shoulder and smiled with a nimbus all around him. The butterflies landed on Marcabrusa's shoulders and head and Volushka thought he heard them singing.

"Get your hands off me! You're lucky we haven't met, I'm going to kill you! I owe you that much from our last encounter! And give me that damned horn, I won't tell you again!"

"You don't owe me anything, consider it all forgotten. Of course, I've missed you, too, but I've been especially busy. You cannot imagine how many people have died and, with rapturous joy, have awakened in the last few weeks, this must be the most cursed and dangerous village on earth. I have been in the cemetery almost exclusively this whole time, really taking in the money, and the villagers have been so sweet, bringing me food and flowers and covers to keep me warm, I can see why you love this job, there's nothing quite like it. The peace of the cemetery, the beautiful reunions at the grave, the lucre, the adoration of the people, I'll never trade it for anything else; why, if they asked me to be Pope, begging to whisk me away on a golden litter to a palace in the clouds, I'd absolutely decline, on the grounds that I've found my craft and Heavenly Grace. Look, I even bought this little ermine scarf!"

"That's it, you've had it! Right now, to the death!"

"Haven't we been through that before? Besides, you look like you've already had your beating today, does that bucket have parts of your face on it? How many old women did this to you?"

"Don't worry how many it was, I've always got plenty for you!"

"Well, that's very generous, of course, and you're a real darling, but I'll have to pass and simply doff my horn, I have to consider now my new and ennobled standing in the village, I can't just engage in dirty street brawls with shitheads and lowlifes, no offense intended, now that I'm a respected and valued member of the higher establishment. That comes with my regrets, of course, and wishes for your continued success."

Volushka charged Marcabrusa, who did a lazy dodge left and let Volushka tumble over himself into the dust. He scrambled to his feet and turned around to charge again and Marcabrusa punched him in the face.

Volushka's head swiveled around in its confused little smoke.

"Look, I'd be very glad to meet up later to punch you in the face again and again, I love the humor, too, but I've been invited for breakfast at Olfa Dodeskaya's, she's invited many of the matrons and young beauties over to entertain me, a sweet gesture, really, and I owe them a morning in kind. I'll be over with the boys at Maroska's farm tonight, I'm bringing over some bracing drink Luska gave me to cheer him up over a horse he lost and we'll have a right old time, why don't you come over then and we can all discuss it like gentlemen? You look a little tired now anyway, I'd be glad to help you to the ground if you want to rest and gather your spirits for later."

Volushka offered a weak, wayward punch in the air and Marcabrusa punched him to the ground.

"Now, you've made my hands all dingy and that's just insensitive on your part, knowing I've a duty to a dainty engagement. At a glance, it almost seems spiteful. … but then there you are, lying in a big, sad lump in all of life's pitiful poverty, how fouled are the engines of human volition. It almost gets my poetry up. Alas! This life is such an awful thing, there's so much lust, sorrow and savagery in it, and I suspect there always will be, craved by the human soul. We can only do the best we can, I suppose, and treasure the little bounties we can scrape… Well, keep scraping, my Little Crumbled One, keep scraping. The Judgment upon us will be terrifying and relentless, so rest now in the mud, sweet, sweet serpent, with your glistering, golden scales."

He walked away with the whistles.

Volushka laid there alone and fuzzy in the streets with his head all mashed up for almost a half hour when he was roused by Cookies sniffing his face.

He smacked the dog in the head and brushed him away, Cookies growling at him and baring his teeth before running off. Volushka staggered over to the well to drink some water and clear his head. He leaned over the well to rest and the butterflies covered him. He was too tired and aggrieved to shoo them away.

"Are you almost done with the well, Sir?"

Volushka splashed some water in his face and turned to see Vulga and Groska with their home buckets and gray workaday smocks.

"I'm sorry, I'm a little bit of a mess, I had to fight off a vampire last night in the graveyard and just barely made it to the dawn…"

"I thought Marcabrusa was our new Grave Listener," Groska said.

"Well, he isn't! And don't go around saying he is! Whatever he's doing up there, it's not Grave Listening and it's against the law! You can be sure that whoever's going into the ground is his fault, and it's only demonic powers, aping Christ, that's raising them out of the graves! You stay away from him if you want to stay safe!"

"Do you know where Benzi is?" Vulga asked.

"I expect he's still at home sleeping in his manger, with the angels and the asses all around him."

"Can you tell him I said Hi?"

"Which one are you?"

"I'm Vulga!"

"Of course, my Principessa, I'm sure he'll be delighted."

"Why do you have so many butterflies all over you?" Groska asked with giggles.

"Well, I'm a friend to animals, I just sent Cookies on his way. I like to take my butterflies to the well to feed and water them and they like to sing little songs in my ears."

"Can I hear one of their songs?" Vulga asked with shy fascination.

"Well, not just anybody can hear them, you must be specially attuned, like Grave Listeners. And most butterflies don't have the strength to sing on just water, or even on the basic floral nectars, which is why I mix in this magical flour in their drink. They like the flour because it makes their colors bright, their hearts feel joy and the nectars in their bellies sweeter. That's why ghosts like to eat them."

"It makes them sweeter?" Vulga asked hopefully.

"It does, it's like honey in your belly and makes you sweeter."

"Then why don't you eat it?"

"That wouldn't work on him!" Groska said with disdainful authority.

"It would work on everybody!"

"Even reprobates?"

"I'm not a reprobate! Do you even know what that is?"

"I think it's like a monster that's part crocodile, part elephant, and part moron."

"Well, it works on everybody! I only give it to my butterflies because they're nice and they like to look pretty in their colorful wings!"

"Can I have some?" Vulga pleaded.

"I can't just give it to everyone, I have to save it for my butterflies. You wouldn't want the butterflies not to look pretty, would you? That's how you get the filthy moths!"

"Please!"

"Well, since you're friends with Benzi, I guess I can give you a little, but just a little — I don't want you to become much prettier than Groska, it will cause people to ignore her and inflame a jealous rivalry between you that will destroy you both. Believe me, I've seen it and it makes monsters out of people."

"Well, I want some, too!"

"I don't have enough to give to the both of you and also feed my butterflies! You're just going to have to be the ugly one for a little while!"

"I can have some of hers!"

"No, you can't, I'm only getting a little!"

"Yes, I can!" And Groska started to cry.

"O, that Heaven made two Eves... Ok, ok, don't cry, I'll give you both some of the flour and I'll give the butterflies some hibiscus later. But don't go around mesmerizing everyone with your beauty, go straight home and don't cause any trouble. You start making everyone foolish and no work will get done, the rest of us will starve to death while the glamorized are bringing you cakes and sweets!"

"We won't cause any trouble, we promise!"

"Ok, well, let me mix the flour in the water in this bucket. This is for you, Vulga...drink it all down, that's good. And this, Groska, is for you…"

After drinking down the powders, the two filled their pails at the well and started off for home, slowly turning pale purple and darkening around their eyes. They ran home excited, beset with dreams that took them far away in their minds.

Volushka slithered off down the street to disappear into the *Uphegia* fields.

And inaudibly to all those unattuned, the butterflies sang, *Sweet Little Gruesome, God of Annihilations,* a butterfly song.

13 RED FLOWER, WHITE FLOWER

The girls made it only quite to their door and collapsed. Their club-footed mother hobbled out in horror to help them and cried out in loud, unending lamentations, drawing all the villagers away from their work, their pretty breakfasts, their convolutions for getting sober from the night before.

Nearly the whole village encircled the family to see what they could do and in their anguish called out again and again for Doctor Klaschke and Marcabrusa, who were already on their way.

Doctor Klaschke forced his way through the circle and kneeled over the girls to examine them. He hung his head wearily in the face of an unending plague for which he had no answers and he sighed with deep pain for another instance of such young and innocent victims. Even if they were to wake, the trauma of the burial, especially for children, froze him. He had recommended again and again that those that appeared affected by the plague remain unburied for a week or two to see if the victims would wake but he could not overcome the religious objections or the greed of the Undertaker's specious arguments, even to spare their loved ones.

When Marcabrusa came, he was ushered into the center of the circle. He knelt beside Doctor Klaschke and commiserated with him.

"The anger of God spares no one. It is especially heavy on the children; I just don't know how to bear up."

"Where there is unrelenting wickedness, there is unrelenting Righteousness," Dr. Klaschke sighed, pale with sorrow.

"Is there anything I can do?"

"I don't know what to do here. Without Father Josep or any response from the Bishop, we have no spiritual recourse. Nothing in my Herbals or in my Authorities is proving effective to ward it off or treat the sickness. Asclepiades doesn't mention it, Galen has been thwarted by it."

The crowd groaned in exasperated sorrow and thrills of fear went round the circle.

"What kind of Doctor are you then exactly?" one of the villagers in the back shouted.

"The kind who is at the limit of this pestilence! If it's a Judgment of God, I'm not going to be able to gainstand it or cause it to swerve! I'm just a man, like you, and in the same predicament!"

"All those fancy books for nothing!"

"If you have an idea, I'd love to hear it!"

The crowd argued among each other, defending the Doctor or assailing his incompetence, while accusing each other as the cause of the plague in a litany of sins, deformities and old grudges. A fight finally broke out between the Blacksmith and Butcher that raised lusty cheers.

Volushka, who had stood a little apart, finally forced his way into the distracted crowd as the fighting came to its sad and bloody conclusion.

"Listen! You can fight with each other or with me, but the reason for this plague, and the way to avert it, is very clear!"

The whole crowd, to the last person, stood in stunned silence at the temerity of this man to even show his face, let alone speak to them. The silence settled ponderously on the entire world so that even the butterflies were quiet. Volushka shifted uncomfortably in the unblinking stares and the hollow nothingness. He resumed at first with an honest diffidence.

"I'm not the authority here, or a respected member, and for whatever I've done, I have no illusions about redemption, I'm just as fearful and agonized as you about what's happening to us all. Life for me wasn't especially good before this visitation and I expect it'll be worse when we emerge from it, but one thing I know is that this village was in a better place before Marcabrusa arrived. Just let me speak — on the surface, he's charming and kind, and it's no mark on anyone if they were gulled by his persuasions. But if you can shake off his glamours, you'll be forced to admit that all of this trouble started when he came to the village; I might even posit that he prepared his demonic way the week before, causing our Father Josep to suffer the dancing sickness right into the bog so that we would be vulnerable to all manner of spiritual attacks. And now we're fighting amongst ourselves and burying children. Everywhere he stalks, he's celebrated for waking the very people he's burying, so that you turn on the only person in the village that is inimical to him and can unmask him. And once I'm destroyed and he has the will of the people, he can then put his heel on your neck. However you feel about it, I am a part of this village and my welfare is in the same jeopardy as yours. I ask then, when is it going to be enough? How many have to go into the ground until we do something about it?"

Marcabrusa interjected with a calm but forceful air.

"I understand fear, too, and what it does to people. If your welfare is in jeopardy, mine is, too, and not only from a terrifying plague but I also have had to suffer and endure the suspicions of the stranger, the aspersions of the jealous, the superstitions of the weak-minded. My conduct has had to be of an almost unearthly character, even as I am a frail man, and afraid, like all of you. To that end, far from casting spells or a glamour, when have I been anything other than humble? When have I refused to help, in any matter, to support this village, building what's needed, sowing and harvesting to feed you, running to every alarm? I have stood with you shoulder to shoulder, risking my life. I tell you it would have been much easier to run away from this sick and accursed village to save myself but, far from me wanting to put my heel on your neck, I simply wanted a small patch to live out my life, among a good people. But if I expect to live among you, then it is right to work with you and carry your burdens; I absolutely have a responsibility to share in your misfortunes before I share your bounty. That is why I am here and it's my only motivation."

Volushka scoffed. "This is all very smooth, and touching, but this is exactly the kind of charming deceit that has led us into our fatal snares! Burials every day, people rising from their graves, discord and vice, what other sorcery do you need to see the truth?"

"What sorcery have I done? This man accuses me because he feels I usurped his place, but you all reviled him long before I arrived, it was you who drove him into the fields, not me. In his absence, I merely offered to help listen at the graves of your loved ones, as one of many offers to help, for every kind of need. My accuser rattles on and on about my devious deceits, my grand designs, but I ask for what? To be a Grave Listener? It is clearly not a profession that is well respected and certainly not something to which I aspire. It's Volushka's entirely, if he is the man for it."

"And what demonic heights do you aspire to?"

"A small hovel, a little sustaining work, a neighborly life."

"That's what he tells *you*, he mocks me to my face with my own tools and tales of his unnatural successes!"

"I am certainly not going to apologize for playing a part if asked in returning people to their loved ones. And I'm not going to apologize if I am better at it than you."

"You're no Grave Listener, you're a sorcerer!"

"I don't claim to have any special expertise, discernment or art, as a matter of fact, it requires no skill at all to be mindful and to listen, it's a job for an idiot. The only requirement it begs is for its Listener not to have a drinking problem."

The crowd rose up in cheers and laughter.

"You filthy son of a bitch! Yet you have no problem accepting all the praise and credit for saving all these people! It's one big tour of gratitude, with free meals and unstinting drinks!"

"Should I disparage the hospitality of a kind people?"

"You should admit you're a fraud and are deceiving these people, burying their loved ones so you can sup on the delights of their hard-earned stores!"

"I would say that you, Sir, are the fraud. *You* are the deceiver in the cemetery, sleeping and drinking, deaf to the dead in your dereliction."

"I challenge you then, here and now, to see who the fraud is and who is the rightful man!"

"I am glad to fight you for my honor and let this crowd

judge us."

"Are you glad to prove you can listen and wake a corpse without sorcery?"

"I am glad to contest you in any way that's proper. But I've already told you I don't have any control over who wakes and who doesn't."

"And I say you do!"

"And how would you like to prove this?"

"Here are two girls of the same age and constitution, who have perished from the same condition, no difference to their very souls, so that there should be no advantage to the one man or the other. I'll listen for Vulga and you'll listen for Groska and with the eyes of God watching us, guided and judged by His devotion to the righteous truth, we will see who the honest man is, the professional Listener, the anointed one who, by his probity and his faith, can effect the salvation of the child under his care!"

"Perhaps you can come up with a sensible way to prove our merits when you're sober."

"I don't need a drink to best you in a righteous fight, I just need my horn and tools back!"

"Well, I can't do any listening without them either."

"I'll make an extra set and bring them to the cemetery," the Blacksmith said, to the cheers of the crowd.

They argued and traded insults for a long time as the crowd's jeering rose wilder and hotter all around them. In the end, as is always the case with human nature, the reasons to hold a contest or not, especially one whose outcome could result in brutality against one or, preferably, both rivals, were meaningless. The prospect of entertainment was too much to pass up.

Volushka sent a knowing glance to the Undertaker as the villagers carried the children to his parlor.

The Undertaker simply scowled in return.

14 THE HORSELEACH HATH TWO DAUGHTERS...

Volushka had to wait until the next morning for the Undertaker to prepare the coffins and dress the bodies, after which that cinereous malcontent would draw the coffins by mules on a sledge up the cemetery hill.

Though invited by some of the men to the tavern, Marcabrusa went off by himself toward the cemetery. Volushka watched him with suspicion, considering it a calculated move to appear to the crowd as contemplative, serious or pious, and he also fretted about any kind of trickery in setting up his position on the hill. He was afraid to follow him directly in case it turned into a brawl, which could settle the matter before it started. The ground was soft at the bottom of the hill, and Volushka would prefer to fight him on the stone roads of Rome or the marble of a Principessa's palace.

Volushka went to the brothel to get a drink and talk with the girls. He wasn't especially in the mood for a rumpfuffle as much as he wanted company, and with Rutchka's hysterical demise, there really wasn't anyone who would sleep with him anyway.

The girls weren't generally busy during the day and the

death of the twins had squelched any lust the village had to offer. Luba and Tulip were playing Scopa, Beskovina and Neva were sharing a lazy drink watching them. Some of the girls were getting some extra sleep upstairs. Petchka was counting money and doing her figures. She reflexively snapped at Volushka, without much conviction or care.

"What are you doing here? Shouldn't you be passed out in the cemetery?"

"I'm not due there until tomorrow, the Undertaker's crafting the girls. It's an important day for me and I'm full of nervous anticipation."

"Nobody here is available for you."

"I just want to talk; I don't have anywhere else to go."

"This isn't a home for vagabonds and sea monsters, it's a place of business."

"I can pay, I'm not expecting charity or human kindness. Can I have a drink?"

"I don't want you getting drunk in here, I have no qualms about taking a chair across your head!"

"I don't have the luxury to get drunk, I have to be sharp for my apocalyptic battle with that bringer of the plague. After I defeat him tomorrow, this whole village will be freed! You'll have business for months with a hale and grateful people."

"I see that you've already been drinking."

"I have not! If you don't want to serve me a drink, I can pay for some company. Just a little conversation to occupy the time before I have to tangle in the dust of the graveyard."

"Go sit down. But if you start bothering the girls, I'm throwing you out."

He sat down at the table and Tulip rolled her eyes.

"Those are some interesting cards."

Luba looked to Petchka to ask by her expression if this was something she had to entertain and Petchka gently nodded.

"I suppose they are. They're foreign."

"I've been to some exotic lands and I've never seen anything like them. I once saw a group of Witches play a game under a full moon in a field of violets with cards pictured with hideous demons and frightful, hellish monsters. Depending on the combination of cards in their hand, they could raise a terrible storm, curse the cattle, cause the village wives to be barren."

The girls started to feel uneasy for playing at cards and tried to ignore him.

"It sent a shiver even to the tips of my hair. But I was almost turned to stone when I realized what they were playing for – between them in the center was a small shape in a burlap sack that began to cry..."

Luba and Tulip both scowled at him.

"I know, it was horrible. I ran as fast as I could all the way to the Cemetery of the Martyrs with the Witches laughing behind me, through a rainstorm conjured from a swarm of midges. I was called to the cemetery for the Marchese of Baciovanco, who died under mysterious circumstances, he was a personal friend of my father. He was no doubt afflicted from the Witches in the area...."

"This is a nice little brothel. That's my great-grandfather's head nailed up there to the rafters, he had become a vampire through no fault of his own and began eating some of the girls here, they cut his head off so he wouldn't continue to walk in the village. It always warms me to see him up there smiling at me.... We could sure use some rain."

"It never rains during an Autumn plague. The air is troubled with phantoms," Tulip said.

"That's true. You can't trust sunny days in Autumn. I could feel the phantoms coming on when I was grave listening for Father Josep and I was thinking that we're in for some bright, unpleasant weather. He was a nice man. Dragging him out of that bog was horrible. His face was all twisted…"

"Please shut up, I don't want any stories about bog corpses!"

"Let us play the hand!"

"Sorry, sometimes I get lost in the tales of the trade. It's not very flattering, I know, and I guess it can be downright gruesome if you don't have the fortitude for it. You think you have the constitution until you see someone's intestines all black and swollen with humors just flopping over their balls."

"For God's sakes! Petchka!"

"What did I tell you?!"

"I'm sorry, I'm all over the place with this combat tomorrow, and as I don't often have a mix of company, I'm untutored in the Graces. I'll be more circumspect, maybe just a little drink will take the steam out of me?"

"I'll give you one if it will keep you quiet. Go sit in the corner and shut up. If you get out of hand, I'm going to pull your skull off!"

It kept him quiet. He only got out of the chair to go to the bar to ask for another little drink to settle him down and because it seemed to be working, and he was paying for it on a slow day, Petchka gave it to him. It helped him suffer his loneliness, in a room full of women, and propped his flagging courage for his showdown with Marcabrusa. He drank them slowly, daydreaming, watching the girls play cards, arguing with himself about life and his prospects. After several hours, and the last of his money, Volushka drifted in and out of sleep.

"If you're done, then get out! I can't have you sleeping in here like some disgusting hippopotamus and turning away all my guests!"

"What guests?"

"The evening guests! Don't push me! I don't want you sickening the clientele!"

"Can I just sleep here for the night? I'll be out by dawn, I have to be at the cemetery early, I want to be there when the bodies arrive."

"Do you have any money left?"

"No, but I will have lots of it once Marcabrusa is vanquished and I have my job back. I'll pay you double for letting me slide."

"I don't have an extra room for you, all the girls need them to work. This isn't an inn!"

"If you don't have the room, why'd you ask if I had any money?"

Petchka marched up to him and grabbed him by the throat. She tried to drag him out of the chair and across the floor but he was too big and he ended up falling on top of her.

"Get the Hell off me! You stink!"

"I will but don't punch me or kick me or any other kind of smashing me in the balls! Look, I don't have anywhere to go, I don't want to spend the night alone in the forest, can you just let me stay here tonight?"

"I don't have a bed for you! I don't know why the Hell I let you in here! …You can sleep in the tub out back. If I can find a pillow and a dirty blanket, I'll let you have them. But don't come back inside and be gone tomorrow before I wake up!"

Volushka went to the back of the brothel and sat in the cold tub. He groused for a while, descended into gales of self-pity and eventually tired himself out, drifting into sleep.

He woke up once in the very early morning to find a pillow and blanket at his feet in the tub. His back and legs were all cramped up as he put the pillow behind him and spread the blanket over. It took him a while, but the pillow and the blanket's warmth finally coaxed him into a very deep dream.

He awoke to a spider eating a cabbage looper on his belly. He laid there, disoriented, the sleep still heavy on his head. The faded sun stung his eyes as it descended on the horizon, and his belly rumbled from ten fathoms deep. He looked around to try and get his bearings and found the brothel was especially quiet.

He knew he promised to leave before Petchka was up but, hungry as he was, he thought he would just peek into the brothel to see if he could put a little food on his tab. The girls didn't always go straight to bed at dawn and would sometimes take a meal at the end of the shift before going to sleep, perhaps they'd give him some without shouting at him or punching him in the face, if only to get rid of him. He wandered in quietly, so as not to wake the Ogress, and poked around the parlor but no one was around. He searched the bar but there wasn't anything to eat. He didn't want a drink so early in the morning, and on such a momentous day, and walked out the front door of the brothel into the street.

As he was walking to the well to get a drink, he felt a very strange feeling, as if something was not quite right. The village was hauntingly empty, mysteriously silent. He'd been the only person awake and in the streets at dawn before, but this quiet felt particularly eerie. The light seemed at once brighter and yet declining, a disjointed, phantasmagorical quality that was spiritually unsettling. Spectres usually returned to their shadows and their lairs in

123

the dawn, but something wicked was certainly about. All of Nature seemed to be off her axis; in the sky, the sun seemed to be in the entirely wrong place. Was this the Revelations at hand? Was this the half hour of silence in Heaven?

Volushka started running as fast as he could to the cemetery on the hill. He had grossly overslept, and it was now five o'clock in the afternoon.

Cookies came out from under the tavern and started running alongside him, barking and jumping on him, until the two tripped over each other and Volushka fell face-first into the dirt. Cookies bit him, Volushka punched him in the head and the two parted shouting at each other.

The whole village was at the top of the hill.

Volushka was in near tears to think that the girls had been buried and that Marcabrusa had chosen his grave. Or, that the crowd at the top of the hill had returned to dig Vulga out of *her* grave in triumph. He huffed up the hill in panic and wondered if he should instead turn around and run out of the village.

When he finally got to the top, he forced his way through the crowd to confront Marcabrusa only to see three coffins side by side and the men finishing a third grave.

The crowd was solemn and hushed.

Volushka looked over the coffins and was dumbstruck with horror to find that none of them had any flowers affixed to them. He searched frantically around the crowd until he saw Benzi holding hands with his sister, smiling, with a red flower in his lapel.

"What the Hell happened?" Volushka asked in despair.

"Wickedness has happened, it has been an unending horror of strange things!" cried Mrs. Saskoveska.

"What the Hell does that mean?"

Fyodor the Butcher spoke up from the third grave. "Maroska Kepkovic's horse, driven by some foul demon, has been wandering elusively all through the town like a ghost. When the Undertaker was putting the coffins on the sledge, the delusional horse approached him from out of a mist, froze like a stone, farted and died, falling right on top of him and crushing him. Marcabrusa with his gifts was somehow able to wake the horse who walked off into the tavern, but the Undertaker was squashed through. We did our best to powder him and make up his clothes and we come up here to bury him with the girls."

Volushka buried his face in his hands and forced back the impulse to cry out. He took a step back to survey the scene and recover himself, finally looking at Marcabrusa. He was startled to see that Marcabrusa had lost all of his confidence, his expression both sullen and worried. Volushka felt the desperate gravity for both of them and was cold with fear.

"Well, there's only two sets of horns, I can't grave-listen for two people here," Volushka said.

"There's no need to listen for him. His head is utterly pulverized and his brains is in his hat," Luska said.

"Which grave is Vulga's?"

"What difference does it make? You just stand there and shut up or we'll dump you in with the Undertaker."

Volushka and Marcabrusa stood quietly as the men buried the three coffins, doing their best to show cold reserves and expressions of stony contemplation to hide their worry. Volushka was accustomed to being in front of an imminent beating, but Marcabrusa could see a wolfish anticipation that, for the first time, included him. When the burials were finally finished, old Ulka Grigorvich, the Farrier, mumbled off a Paternoster and the crowd departed down the hill.

Marcabrusa refused to look at Volushka. He attached his horn to the stop plate tube sticking out of the ground and sat down at the grave, shaking his head in disgust.

Volushka felt the insult. "You know, you could just run away, go to a new village. You don't have to go through with this. It would probably be better for you if you did. These people will turn on you just for the boredom."

"It's the same thing in every poor, superstitious shithole in the land; I've been run out of every place I've been to, and I barely got out of the last one alive. Everywhere you go is just a village of animal idiots. Human nature is always the same. It may be easier to disappear in the big cities but the gangs are larger and more fierce, there are ranging diseases, desperate poverty, brutal soldiers, and corruption in the high places. If you want to run away, be my guest but I've seen it, there's nowhere to go."

"With all your charms, you'd have a better chance of it than most, more than me at least."

"All my charm has landed me sitting on a grave."

"Well, it's your own fault, nobody asked you to come here!"

"When I saw how stupid and grotesque you are, I thought I'd finally found a place to settle, I thought it would be easy to toss you aside and set up a decent, easy living but I didn't count on the depths of how dumb you really are. This ridiculous plan of yours will expose us both and get us killed. Neither of us can wake anyone and you know it. Why the Hell would you give them that idea when they were dumb enough to pay us otherwise?"

"Maybe we can, maybe not. But you're the one that pushed it too far, they even think you woke a horse!"

"Don't talk to me."

The two men sat in gloomy, seething silence as the sun set behind them over the village.

They were awake all night, afraid of being murdered by their rival in their sleep. Volushka was not only listening at his horn but furtively leaning over to listen at Marcabrusa's to see if Vulga was in his grave. He'd make exaggerated stretches toward Marcabrusa's side or walk behind his horn to see if he could hear anything, and it made Marcabrusa suspicious. He began listening intently at his own horn, and then also listening at Volushka's. They squared up to claim their graves and then guarded their own space fiercely.

As the sun came up, both men were hungry and exhausted, and had few reserves left on which to endure. Just before it erupted into a fatal fight, Magaden and Tulip came up the hill with food and some blossom wine.

"Anything yet?" Magaden asked with worry.

"No," Marcabrusa said quietly.

"Please just try. They're just little girls."

"We'll do everything we can," Volushka said heroically but the girls just dismissed him with a glance.

Addressing Marcabrusa, Tulip said, "Luska will bring some food tonight and some extra drink for the chill." The girls then left.

By the late afternoon, both men were drifting off to sleep. Benzi and Bunny had snuck into the graveyard at lunchtime to watch them, first running into the stand of trees at the back of the hill and then, as they nodded off, hiding behind a nearby headstone. He threw a little pebble at Volushka which hit him in the head and awakened him in a panic, which made Benzi quietly giggle. When he realized that he wasn't being attacked by Marcabrusa or a Vrykolakas, he slumped back down into the dirt to nap. Long before night came, the tedium of watching these two do nothing but snore coupled with the peace of the girls resting in their eternal corruption tuckered Benzi out. He laid down on Bunny and went to sleep behind the headstone and now everyone in the cemetery was in the land of dreams.

When the two men woke, there was food and blossom wine at their feet. Marcabrusa was not used to sleeping on the ground, invited as he was into every home, and so twisted himself to try to stretch the cramps out of his neck and back. Volushka had no such unfamiliar aches.

Marcabrusa looked out over the village solemnly. "Is anyone going to stop that damned sexton from ringing that bell? ...At some point, we may have to pronounce them dead and then deal with our reckoning. At any rate, I'm not keen to be here for five days sleeping in the dirt with you."

"Are you keen to have your reckoning?"

"These people are pretty stupid. I'll take my chances handling them."

"Well, I'm in no hurry."

"I wouldn't expect you would be."

"We've a few days at least to come up with something, depending on what happens at your grave or mine."

"There's no *we* about it. You're on your own."

"Well, don't you worry about me, I can handle myself, and you! I'm going to take a piss, feel free to run off like a coward if you'd like, I'll take care of both of the girls."

Volushka picked up his share of the food and some blossom wine and walked to the last row of graves before the woods and pissed all over the back of old Priska Wlawicka's headstone.

He returned to find Marcabrusa on alert, excited, listening intently into his horn. Volushka was white with fear.

"What do you hear? What is it?!"

"Shut the Hell up!"

Volushka listened over his shoulder but couldn't hear anything. Marcabrusa turned on Volushka and shoved him to the ground.

"Get the Hell off of me!" he shouted and stood over Volushka with a wild look. He then returned to the horn, straining to hear.

Volushka stayed on the ground, watching and waiting. He couldn't hear anything, or maybe he could, perhaps a tapping, or was there a voice? A light breeze seemed to sweep up the graveyard and confuse everything. Without getting to the horn, it was hard to know for sure.

Marcabrusa was fixed to the horn, practically inserting his head into it. The silence and the tension froze each man into their spot.

Suddenly, breaking into a wide, maniacal smile, Marcabrusa started laughing and shouting, erupting into howls of excitement. He turned to Volushka with a victorious look and then ran down the hill toward the village, leaping, spinning and dancing as he descended.

Volushka was horrified. He ran to the horn and listened for any kind of sound but couldn't hear anything at all. He shouted into the horn but no response returned. What could he have possibly heard? There was absolutely nothing. He listened with desperation but nothing came back to him at all.

Benzi awakened when Marcabrusa rejoiced. He watched him run down the hill and saw Volushka's despairing worry and he became afraid for Volushka. He knew the villagers would be coming soon, and his Uncle and his sisters, so he ran out from behind the headstone, into the woods to hide. He knew that they would look in his bed for him and he wouldn't be there yet again, which would mean his Uncle would shout at him and threaten to strap him until his sisters shielded him and turned his Uncle's wrath away. Then his sisters would scold him, and if he cried, give him a cookie. He reckoned it would be better to sneak out through the woods and back into the village, as close to his house as he could get; if they found him in the cemetery, there would probably be no cookie at the end.

Just as Benzi was about to dart off through the woods, he could hear Volushka start to become hysterical, switching ears at Marcabrusa's horn to find any kind of sound, then jumping back and forth between that horn and his own. He watched him in his apish panic with fascination and worry.

Volushka stomped around slapping himself in the head with anxiety and frustration. He could see Marcabrusa far in the distance running down the street and had no idea where to go or what to do. In his panic, he finally poured all of the Witch's powder down Marcabrusa's horn in the desperate hope that it would re-poison her and extend the resemblance of death until well after the villagers disinterred her. When he ran out of the powder, he started throwing sand down the horn. He shook the horn and the tube and then started blowing into it to try and get all of the powder down into the grave.

At that very same moment, in the awful little hut in the bogs, the Witch of Gore Mal Gore hummed as she pestled the liver of a little boy in a small, golden bowl, when the hut in an instant became freezing cold, and a Great Shadow formed out of the air behind her. A black tail slithered around her body and finally encircled her neck and began to strangle her. The Witch dropped her pestle and struggled to free herself when she froze in a vision.

"No, Master! No! Please! Not Volushka! Please, my Lord, not him…" The Great Shadow strangled her to the ground and the hut began to burn.

Volushka stopped to catch his breath and then blew as hard as he could into the horn to push the Witch's powder down the tube. He blew a second time and then he took his deepest breath and blew again.

Out of the horn exploded a terrific fireball, which blew back into his face and down his body. It started an absolutely infernal, magical conflagration that blazed out in all directions, fast and high and violent, engulfing in an instant the greater part of the cemetery on the hill. Volushka screamed ceaselessly, convulsing in the fire, slapping at his face to try to put it out, falling to the ground, writhing in grotesque agony.

Benzi was blown backward by the blast and began screaming, too. He called out for Volushka desperately and as he listened to Volushka howling in pain, he began to cry. He looked for Volushka through the wall of fire and when he finally saw him, rolling around in spasms of torture, he covered his face with Bunny and ran into the cemetery through a little gap in the flame.

When he reached Volushka, Benzi kicked dirt on him. He cried out in his tears, "It's me, Benzi! It's me! Hold on!"

He grabbed Volushka by the burned away rags of his coat to try and drag him out of the cemetery but Volushka was too heavy. "Please get up, Volushka!"

Volushka garbled through the fire engulfing his face and his burned away tongue, "Benzi, get out of here! Run! RUN!!"

Benzi looked into his horrible, scorched away face and screamed in terror. He ran away as fast as he could, in and out of the smoke and the flames, toward where he thought the cemetery gates would be. The flames sprung up all around him and blocked his path, surrounding the crown of the hill, and he got lost, crying out for Volushka who by now was completely blind.

"Benzi, where are you? I'll get you! Where are you?? Come to me, follow my voice! Run, Benzi, as fast as you can! I'm over here, come to me over here!!"

Benzi, hemmed in by the flames, finally just ran in a random direction as fast as he could. As he ran, he looked back for Volushka, calling his name, and in doing so, ran into the horizontal stone beam of a cross-shaped headstone. He hit his head a little behind his right ear and fell backward into the grass with such force, Bunny was thrown out of his hand along with the Witch's gift, the skull with the long black hair he had kept in his pocket. Benzi lay there small in the grass, unconscious and bleeding, until the flames finally enveloped him.

His feet in their little buckled shoes curled up in the fire.

Volushka, blind, on fire and lost, wandered in circles around the cemetery calling out madly and hopelessly for Benzi until he fell at last to the excruciating flames with all his sorrow and worry on his lips.

At the grave of Vulga Bulgy-Ogrova, the horn at Volushka's grave, a little voice woke from the cramped, strangling darkness and in tears and agonized terror, through the dirt that poured in through the coffin lid, cried out for her mother.

As she cried and she screamed and pushed desperately on the coffin lid, the flames burned over the horn until it finally crumpled like a twisting black flower, fell into the dirt and blew away in ashes. With the embers of the horn, her cries vanished from the earth into a deep and placid silence, shrouded by the roaring of the flames.

Despite all the villagers could do, they had to work and live and wait six days in fear for the diabolic fire to subside.

It took the same six days for the little girl to die in tears in that dark, airless grave, covered in dirt, worms and flesh flies, desperately shrieking, shrieking, shrieking underneath our usual lives.

ABOUT THE AUTHOR

William Frank, an author of eight books of poetry, is a man with an amiable façade, a witless disregard for reasonable care and a personal nimbus almost nine feet high. His poetry has previously appeared in *The Dillydoun Review*, the 2022 and the 2023 Bards Annual and he was a runner-up for the 2008 Discovery/The Boston Review prize offered by the 92nd Street Y.

This is his first novel.

When not writing, he enjoys long hours of losing at chess, bingeing on 1950's Japanese Cinema, summering with the Devil, punching cryptids in the face and Kulning.